Getting Lucky with Luciano

by
Kelley Nyrae

Parker Publishing LLC

NOIRE PASSION is an imprint of Parker Publishing LLC.

Copyright © 2008 by Kelley Nyrae
Published by Parker Publishing LLC
12523 Limonite Ave., Ste. #440-438
Mira Loma, California 91752
www.parker-publishing.com

This book is a work of fiction. Characters, names, locations, events and incidents (in either a contemporary and/or historical setting) are products of the author's imagination and are being used in an imaginative manner as par of this work of fiction. Any resemblance to actual events, locations, settings or persons, living or dead, is entirely coincidental.

ISBN: 978-1-60043-028-2
First Edition

Manufactured in the United State of America

Cover Design by Jaxadora Design

Chapter One

Damn, it sucks being the dependable one, Kaylee Daniels thought while sitting at 'their' table at *Luciano's*. Fingering her caramel colored braids she people watched while waiting for her compulsively late friends, Tabby and Bri to arrive. The hustle and bustle of workers and patrons helped her bide her time.

Sitting in the high-class, San Francisco restaurant alone for half an hour could put a serious dent in a girl's ego. A few new faces stared at her. Luckily the regulars knew she was waiting for her tardy friends.

Why couldn't Tabby and Bri be on time at least once? Being late was their trademark. Kaylee could either take it or leave it. And after all they'd been through together, she'd much rather take it. Her two crazy friends were always there when the shit hit the fan. In Kaylee's life, there had been a lot of shit, and one of those enormous wind machine fans.

Duck and cover was her motto. As an adult, Kaylee learned to do a whole lot of ducking and covering to keep her life from being overtaken with the 'mess' that had been hurled her way. As a child, she had to live in it. Not anymore.

At the next table Kaylee watched as a pair of lovers held hands across the deep red tablecloth. A bottle of wine sat next to the three burning candles at the center of their table. They looked to be around her own twenty-eight years. The brunette woman's smile lit the room as she looked into the eyes of her date. Kaylee's heart thumped wildly against her chest as the man pulled out a ring and placed it on the woman's finger. *Lucky lady*, she thought. *No, scratch that, run while you can girl, is more like it.*

The Daniels women were cursed in love, at least that's what her mom always said. Kaylee didn't know for sure about any curses, but what she did know about love made her steer clear.

It looked about as fun as getting teeth pulled without the pain medication. There aren't any shots to numb your heart.

Her mom had been in 'love' enough times in her life for the both of them. After witnessing all of her heart aches Kaylee kept her distance from love.

Unfortunately steering clear of love meant she usually kept her distance from men. No men meant no sex. *Damn I miss sex.*

The sweet smell of basil tickled her senses. She savored the delicious scent while she continued to glance about the restaurant. Over each red-clothed table hung small crystal chandeliers. They looked elegant, yet contemporary. The lights were dimmed to perfection. *Luciano's* was the best place to bring a date, not that she'd know. But it was also a hip place for people to just hang out.

A spur of the moment decision six months ago transpired into what is now known as Friday's at *Luciano's*. Who wanted to wait for a man to take a girl out to a nice dinner? Not in this century. Girl's night out beat a manfest any day. That was until Luciano Valenti walked his fine self into the picture. The man himself said yummy better than the gourmet Italian food he sold in his restaurant. Not that the food wasn't great, he was just better. Everything about him set her body cooking. The man sizzled.

Luciano threw all Kaylee's "stay away from men" rules right out the window. He made her want to attack him like a sex-crazed lunatic. Kaylee didn't do sex-crazed lunatic, at least she hadn't until she met Luciano.

As long as he didn't come within touching distance she could handle it. The first two months were a breeze. Then, Nico, Luciano's cousin and head chef noticed Tabby. A flirt and a half, he started spending more and more time around their table; chatting, winking and smiling at Tabby every chance he got. Then Luciano joined in the visiting sessions and things were never the same.

What started out as a little extra dessert or appetizer here and there turned into Nico bringing out whatever new recipe he had in the works. Kaylee, Bri, and Tabby would try it out and give him their opinion. While they ate their food, Nico and Luciano pulled up their own chairs and joined them.

You'd think spending time around the object of your attraction would be a good thing. Nope, not with Kaylee.

Each time Luciano approached the table, he seemed so intense. His mysterious dark eyes zeroed in on her. When Luciano made an appearance she went into lust overdrive, and became a stammering klutz. She couldn't get within a couple feet of Luciano without spilling, dropping, or hitting something.

The Daniels' curse strikes again. All she wanted was a chance to chill with the guy and admire that fine physique of his. She may not be able to touch but she sure as hell could ogle. The man won the award for San Francisco's finest, hands down. After a hard day at her bookstore, Kaylee deserved to do a little looking.

The bell over the door jingled. Kaylee looked across the packed restaurant to see if her friends had arrived. *Of course not, that would only make them twenty minutes late.*

She watched as the hostess sat the elderly couple who just entered when suddenly she got the feeling. Luciano must be near by. Goose bumps spread across her already tingling skin. Her heart started beating double time.

She didn't see Luciano yet. But she heard him making rounds like he did every night, greeting his customers in that sexy, baritone voice.

Turning to the left, her hand slid across the table. Just as he approached her, Kaylee did what she always did when he was around, something stupid. As her water glass tipped over creating a small pool on her table, she fought the overwhelming urge to crawl under that same table and hide. *He must think I'm the world's biggest klutz!*

"I'll get that for you," Luciano said as he cleaned the small amount of water with one hand and a napkin. "Luckily you drank most of it already."

His rich, smooth tone wrapped around her making her dizzy. Or maybe that was from the lack of oxygen getting to her brain. Something about being around this man severed all her control over her body. The only connection that never failed was the one to her raging hormones.

"Yeah, lucky me," Kaylee mumbled as she ran her hand up her arm. The heat from his closeness snaked across her bare skin.

"Nico sent out another dessert for you to try while you're waiting for your friends." Luciano set a plate with three pieces of chocolate cake on the table. They looked almost as yummy as Luciano himself.

Taking another quick glance towards Luciano, Kaylee tried to respond but couldn't raise her eyes to look the man in the face. She was nearly eye level with his crotch and couldn't for the life of her turn away. He obviously packed a pretty big bulge beneath his black slacks. Damned if her tongue didn't have a mind of its own and slowly licked her lips. *Get a grip, girl. You're staring at the man's crotch.* Look up. Come on, you can do it.

The view on the way up was just as dangerous as the one below his belt. Flat stomach, *keep going*, broad chest, *you're almost there*, square jaw, knowing smile, and near black colored eyes, *exhale breath, you made it. Wait, knowing smile? Damn, he knows I'm checking him out!*

"Look good?" Luciano said his smile growing.

Kaylee couldn't breathe, much less speak, so she did what she did best when Luciano was around, she stared.

"The dessert," he said. "Does it look good?"

Dessert? What dessert? "Yes. It looks wonderful."

"I'll be sure to tell Nico you said so. We'll be out later with dinner."

He stood there, locking eyes with her, in the process, stopping the beat of her heart a few seconds longer. Then he turned and walked away. She'd need a big dose of Nico's chocolate to jump start her heart.

Kaylee watched Luciano's really tight back side saunter from the room. Good God, the man probably thought she had some serious problems with all the staring and spilling things she did when he was around. But how could a girl stop? With his rich, olive skin and raven hair, he mesmerized her. Pre-Luciano, men with long hair didn't do it for her. The way his black, shiny hair rested on his collar made her imagine how it would feel to run her fingers through it. Many a night in her dreams she'd wrapped the strands around her fingers. His dark hair looked beautiful against her mocha skin.

He towered over her with a long, lean physique that went on for days. None of those things compared to his eyes, nothing beat what those eyes did to her. She got lost in their almost black depths every time. They were dark as night but every so often she noticed a twinkle in them like the first star in the evening sky. *You are seriously losing it, girlfriend.*

Kaylee glanced at the silver watch on her wrist. 7:28. The girls should be here any minute which is exactly what she needed; a little something to get her mind off her Italian dream. Remembering the dessert Luciano brought out for her, she picked up the small square and took a bite. Chocolate, and damn it tasted good. Just like everything Nico made. He could cook like nobody's business.

The bell over the restaurant door jingled, jarring Kaylee from her near chocolate induced orgasm. Following the sound of loud, joyful laughter, Kaylee looked toward her friends.

Though Bri wasn't a typical beauty, she commanded attention. She stood shorter than herself or Tabby, at about 5 foot 3 inches. She kept her hair natural and trimmed in a perfectly rounded afro. Everyone noticed when she walked into a room, and she reveled in that attention. She was the party girl of the group, hated commitment and swore never to settle down until she was too old to keep up with her current pace. Brianna was in the process of buying a coffee shop. The chick could drink caffeine 24/7.

Tabby was the beauty of the group, tall, leggy and trim. Her hair, permed on a regular basis was long and shiny. She always wore the latest styles. Being such a beauty, she was asked out all the time, but mostly by men who thought with their dicks rather than their brains. Her man-picker was broken and had been for a long time. Despite all the pain Tabby continued to look for love. A romantic at heart, she wanted nothing more than to settle down with her knight in shining armor. Tabby was an interior decorator.

"Hey, Kay. Are you sitting there dreaming about the Italian Stud again?" Brianna smiled and nudged Tabby with her elbow. "You hear that? Hey, Kay. I'm a poet and I didn't know it."

She again laughed her contagious laugh. But today, Kaylee was immune. "Shh," Kaylee said, "For God's sake, Bri, could you speak a little louder? I don't think he heard you!"

"Calm down, Kay." Tabby pulled out her chair to sit down. "He isn't even in the room."

"That's not the point. Other people could have heard." Kaylee grabbed for her friend's glass of water and took a drink.

"And they would automatically know who I'm talking about?" Brianna asked. "Give me back my water. If you're going to be all grumpy on me, I'm not going to share."

Kaylee and Tabby both giggled before Kaylee said, "It's impossible to stay mad at you, you know that, Bri?"

"That's just because you love me so much, Kay. Well, that and my undeniable charm," Bri replied.

"Hmm. I somehow missed your charm. I'm glad you guys finally showed up though." Kaylee looked at her two friends.

"You know we'll be late, Kay, so why do you still come so early?" Brianna asked. Before Kaylee had the chance to reply Brianna added, "Never mind, I know you come early so you have more time to ogle Luciano the Italian Stud."

Kaylee would have been irate but Bri had dropped her tone to a whisper so no one would hear her. Plus, she was right. Kaylee came early so she'd have more time to gawk at Luciano. How pathetic was that? *Better not admit to that sour truth.* "Because that's what I do, Bri. If I'm supposed to meet someone at 7:00, I'm there at 7:00." Then remembering what else Bri said, she added, "Where the hell do you come up with these names, anyway?"

"Girl, you know that's what you think of him, isn't it?" Tabby added. "The Italian stud?"

"No. Well, maybe."

All three girls laughed together. *Thank God it's Friday.* With the busy schedule Kaylee kept at her bookstore, Friday was the only night she allowed herself to let loose and actually leave *Bookends* on time. Other than her girl's night out, she dedicated her life to her store.

A moment later the waiter brought the three girls their martinis. Having the waiter bring out a drink without taking the order told Kaylee she spent too much time at *Luciano's*. Why break the habit now?

They had a routine, one drink, girl talk, and then Nico and Luciano usually made their way out with their food. The girl talk was always her favorite. They each drank their apple martini and talked about their day while waiting for Nico to bring out tonight's masterpiece.

"Did you go on a date with what's-his-butt?" Bri asked but quickly changed her wording because of the immediate scowl she received from Tabby. "I mean Michael."

"Yeah, the date started out great. He took me to a fantastic restaurant and was a complete gentleman the entire time. We went out for ice-cream then a walk in the park. I really thought he could be the one. Then he brought me home and I figured he deserved a nice little kiss.

"I guess he had something else in mind. The kiss went from zero to sixty in about five seconds. If I had been a car, it might be okay, but he just couldn't keep his hands off me. I told him it was time to call it a night and he said, and I quote "Too bad women like you waste the beautiful body God gave you." Can you believe that?"

Poor Tabby, Kaylee thought. Looking for love always seemed to get her into trouble.

"Yeah," Bri scolded her. "If you're thinking a guy is "the one" during the first date, something is bound to go wrong. It's about time you learned that."

"Bri! Lay-off, would ya?" Kaylee said before turning her attention back to her other friend. "Ignore her, Tab."

"Good evening ladies," a man's voice said. "How's your night going so far?"

Luciano.

Tabby and Bri both looked at Kaylee waiting for her to reply. After a few seconds she realized they weren't going to answer him, and replied, "It's been great. Thank you." *Not too bad. I actually formed an intelligent sentence.*

"I see Nico hasn't been out with your food yet. I thought I was running late."

"You mean Nico hasn't been out to flirt with Tabby yet."

Leave it to Bri to say the first thing that popped into her mind Kaylee thought.

"Flirting's Nico's nature," Luciano said. "He flirts with all women; but Tabby is his favorite."

Speaking of the devil, Nico made his way from the kitchen in his white chef attire, plates in hand. Nico was almost as tall as Luciano, with the same black hair, except his was cut short and always mussed from his chef's hat. His eyes were dark, with long, black eye lashes. He didn't light Kaylee's fires like Luciano did, but he was a very beautiful man.

As he approached the table, Luciano turned and grabbed two extra chairs from an empty table next to them.

"If it isn't the three women of my dreams," Nico said coming to a stop next to Tabby at the table. "Are you ready to eat?" Nico set a plate in front of each lady while Luciano sat the two extra chairs at their small table. One right next to her.

"What'd you bring out for us tonight, super chef?" Bri asked while the men took the extra seats.

Luciano's leg brushed against Kaylee's as he sat down. Her lips parted almost letting a moan escape. The simplest touch from him set her afire.

"Manicottis," Nico said to Bri before turning to Tabby. "You know, cooking isn't the only thing I've been called super at."

"You are so bad, Nico. Lines like that don't work on me."

Kaylee noticed Tabby didn't look as sure as she tried to sound.

"Eat up, ladies," Luciano jumped into the conversation. "My head chef has to get back to work soon. It's been a busy night."

In just the six months they'd been coming Kaylee noticed a rise in patrons that frequented the establishment on Friday nights.

Nico and Luciano usually spent about thirty minutes with them. Nico tried out a different recipe on Kaylee and her friends each night, while Luciano sat there making her nervous with his intense stare. No one man should ever have as much control over a woman as Luciano had over her. Luckily, it was just her libido he affected. He wouldn't be safe otherwise.

"Dig in before the boss starts cracking the whip, ladies," Nico said with humor in his tone.

Kaylee dug her fork into the delicious looking food on her plate and took a bite. As usual it was divine. The sweet taste of the sauce, the rich cheeses, it was warm and gooey and yummy.

"These cheeses are so rich and creamy," Kaylee said before she could stop herself.

"Rich and creamy is good," Luciano replied. His voice sounded tense.

Heat rushed to her cheeks. From the look on his face Luciano had something else in mind other than the food.

Uh, oh. I'm in serious trouble, Kaylee thought.

"And moist too," Bri played on the words as well. Thank God for great friends. Kaylee didn't know how to reply to the obvious sexual undertones in the conversation. She hadn't meant for it to come out that way, but it had. Leave it to her to say something provocative. Why did he have that affect on her? Ms. Cool, calm and collected turned into a stammering fool around her Italian stud.

"Creamy and moist? Have I told you ladies how much I love you?" Nico turned to Tabby. "What do you think, sweetheart?"

To Kaylee's surprise, Tabby played along. "It's smooth, so smooth, it just melts in my mouth. I think I might need more."

Kaylee turned to Nico then Luciano. They both seemed tense, and if she didn't know better, she'd think they were both pretty damn turned on.

But why was Luciano staring at her? No, it couldn't be desire she saw in his face. Why wouldn't his attention be on Tabby? She was the man magnet of the group. Whatever the reason, his heated gaze gave Kaylee a meltdown of her own. She reached for her water and slowly took a drink, aware of Luciano still watching her.

Bri hit the table. "OK girls. You better quit before you give these two big Italian men orgasms right here at the restaurant."

Kaylee almost choked on her water.

Luciano winked at her.

And damned if she didn't drop the glass, spilling water all over the table for the second time in one night.

Crawling under the table started to sound better and better. The control she fought so strongly to hold on to all but evaporated around Luciano. She depended on the control and the fact that she lost it around him left her uneasy.

"Let me grab a towel and I'll get this cleaned up," Luciano said rising from the table.

Nico, as if knowing exactly what went through her mind, shook his head as he moved one of the heavy, white plates from the table which had water beneath it. All Kaylee could do was hide her face behind her increasingly shaky hands.

After Luciano returned to wipe up Kaylee's mess, the party was obviously over. He and Nico said their goodbyes before heading back to work. Nico hurried back to the kitchen while Luciano disappeared someplace down the hall.

"Tell me I'm dreaming," Kaylee whispered. "Did I really just do that? Again."

"I'm afraid so, sweetie." Tabby patted her hand.

"What do you mean again?" Bri asked at the same time.

Ignoring Bri's question, Kaylee rubbed her eyes before looking at her friends. "Why did they have to start coming out to sit with us every Friday night? It messes everything up. It's much easier to lust after him from afar then it is when he sits at the table with us."

"Calm down, Kay. It wasn't so bad," Bri tried to reassure her. "If it helps, he was totally checking you out before you threw your glass of water at the table."

"Thanks, Bri, that really helped." Kaylee buried her face in her hands.

"Okay, I hate to do this tonight, but you two need some help." Both Kaylee and Tabby looked at Bri while she continued.

"Seriously, Kaylee, you're twenty-eight years old and you're happier lusting after someone from afar than getting the chance to go for him?"

"What's wrong with that?"

"I love you girl, but that isn't normal."

Bri didn't understand. She never had. "I have a business. I have a responsibility. You know that's more important to me than a relationship with a man," Kaylee answered.

"I know you're busy with your bookstore, and you have all those "Daniel's Curse" fears because of your mom, but live a little. I'm not saying you should try and marry the guy, but he's hot, available, and a man. It won't be that hard for you to have a little fun with him. Grow some balls and ask the guy out."

"She might be right, Kay," Tabby jumped in and said. "You never date."

Bri then turned her attention to Tabby.

"Tabby, you know I love you too, girl, but you need to stop focusing on trying to find *the one* with every guy you go out with. You're gorgeous. Lots of men are going to ask you out and 99.9% will be losers. Remember that. Just try and have a little fun, and start with that hunky chef that can't keep his eyes off you."

"Do you guys really think it's normal for the chef and restaurant owner to send out special food and get so chummy with their customers?" On a roll, Bri continued. "Wake up and smell the hot Italian lust. They're seriously feelin' you guys. I'm sorry if I sound harsh, but you two need to learn to stop taking life so seriously!" Bri smiled then said, "Now that I have that off my chest, let's finish this delicious food."

As the evening progressed, Kaylee's thoughts stayed with Bri and what she'd said. Everything she said was the truth, which made her words sting more. Thinking of herself as an old prude didn't sit well, but she knew that's what she was. The alternative was too scary to think about right now. Tomorrow, she'd think about it tomorrow.

The next day as Kaylee meandered down the isles of the grocery store after work, Brianna's words began running through her head again. Somehow she'd pressed the repeat button on her thoughts giving her the mother of all headaches. They'd been plaguing her since the night before.

Live a little. Stop taking life so seriously. The truth of the matter was, it wasn't just Brianna who'd made similar comments to her. If that were the case it would have been easier to ignore. Oh no, today she had seventy year old Martha London in her store talking about her latest date.

As a regular customer Martha felt comfortable talking to Kaylee about a lot of things including her dating habits, then commenting on how Kaylee should be out there getting the "lay of the land" herself. Apparently good old Martha believed you should test drive multiple vehicles before you made a purchase.

Hmm, maybe she was onto something. She wouldn't mind getting the "lay of Luciano's land." Kaylee laughed to herself at her thoughts, but the truth was, it really wasn't all that funny.

I'm a twenty-eight year old, single business owner. Martha London gets more play than I do! Sure she didn't ever plan on settling down with a man. But that didn't mean she couldn't take a few rides around the block. She might not be a beauty like Tabby, or a guaranteed good time like Bri, but she knew she looked okay. Men did ask her out from time to time.

Not that she ever said yes. Her dates were few and far between. Come to think about it in the year since she opened *Bookends*, rare wasn't a strong enough word. Unfortunately for her body, nonexistent fit better. *Live a little. Stop taking life so seriously.*

Logically speaking, that had to be the reason the Italian Stud got to her so badly. Her body was screaming for a little skin on skin contact you just couldn't achieve solo. Continuing to walk up and down the aisles Kaylee let her mind work things out. Always the logical one, she longed for stability in her life. Growing up, stability was unheard of, yet as an adult it was a requirement.

Lusting after Luciano made her feel off balance, out of control, both unacceptable in Kaylee's book. Around Luciano, she rode a never-ending roller coaster. Her body wanted him and that felt exciting, exhilarating and at the same time it scared her. Throw in the fact that her IQ and ability to act as a normal twenty-eight year old woman should, dropped considerably in his presence. She knew she should be running for the hills.

Yet here she was, walking down the aisles at the grocery store wondering if there was a way to have her cake and eat it too. Brianna had been right. She did need to liven up her life. Just because she would never let herself fall in love didn't mean she had to be an old hag who had no fun. Luciano could be a whole lot of fun. The time had come for Kaylee to have some fun. To enjoy herself with a specific Italian

Stud.

It's amazing the clarity that comes from walking around the grocery store.

She was due for an affair.

Due for sex.

Due for Luciano.

Chapter Two

After the enlightening trip to the grocery store, Kaylee put her plan into action. Operation Seduce Luciano was a go. Her plan, to kill two birds with one stone. Seducing Luciano would be a first for her. Hell, seducing anyone would be a first. But it would also add a little spice to her life, something she needed.

Second, she could get Luciano out of her system. Vowing never to date the same person more than a couple times at a young age, Kaylee had yet to feel the urge to break the routine. This would be no different. After she had her fill of him, she'd be able to go on with the business of life. No more lust, no more attack of the killer klutz, no more yearning to have someone so bad you can't see straight.

Sunday Kaylee made a quick appointment to get her hair done that evening. Luckily her hair dresser loved her and gave her a late appointment on short notice. But she knew she would, that's why she spent half Saturday night rubbing her fingers raw, unbraiding her hair. Now as Holly pulled and tugged on her head she had nothing to do but think, think about Luciano, her store, the possibility that she'd make a huge fool of herself. *Don't think about it.*

"I think this red is going to look really good in your hair, girl," her longtime hair dresser said while braiding away. At the last minute, Kaylee decided to throw a little bit of red in with her brown creating a color she liked to call, chocolate cherries.

"Thanks. I hope so," Kaylee replied to her before picking up her latest book to try and get some reading in. She owned a bookstore but never had time to read, if that made any sense at all.

Around 11:00 PM, hair freshly braided, Kaylee made her way back to the apartment she lived in above *Bookends*. Tomorrow started another crazy week at the store and the countdown to Friday began.

Time was screwing with her. Each day passed by faster than the one before until here she was on Thursday night cleaning the floor of her cranberry and green bathroom with a toothbrush, the smell of bleach burning her nose.

This all sounded like such a great plan on Saturday. Sunday it was a good plan, Monday an okay plan, and by today, Thursday it plain sucked. How the hell could she seduce Luciano when she had trouble forming sentences in his presence? Kaylee stood. She needed to call Bri. Her bare feet padded on the hardwood floors as she walked to the phone. She picked it up then immediately put it down. Just because she couldn't sleep, didn't mean Bri shouldn't.

She knew that wasn't really the reason she didn't call. When she told them about Operation: Seduce Luciano, she left out a few of the gory details. All they knew was that she'd finally planned to go for him. They had no idea it was just for a bit of sex and excitement. That usually fell in Bri's territory, and part of Kaylee was still shocked she planned to go there.

Needing sleep she climbed into bed around 3:15 only to toss and turn, nervousness attacking her limbs. No doubt this would be a long night. Well, morning was more like it.

Luciano couldn't believe the dishwasher broke on a Friday night. The specials had to be changed at the last minute due to a disastrous pesto incident, all of this with a packed restaurant and no Nico until 7:00pm. *Perfect night for Nico to take extra time off.* The day chef couldn't match Nico's speed and upbeat attitude in the kitchen. Working on the dishwasher would likely take most of the evening which meant the chances of going out and talking with Kaylee slim to none. Tonight sucked!

Luciano liked the shy, little perfectionist. She was a breath of fresh air compared to most of the women he knew. Something about her caught his attention and had yet to let go. Luciano wanted to wrap her silky braids around his fingers. Her hair must look just as good when she rolled out of bed in the morning. Damn he wanted to test his theory to be sure.

The way her sultry, light brown eyes lingered on his body made it near impossible not to go caveman on her. All he wanted to do was throw her over his shoulder and take her into his back office at the restaurant. He craved her full, kissable lips. All he could think about was licking her milk chocolate skin. Her curvaceous body made his cock pulse with desire.

Kaylee had the perfect figure, luscious and womanly. She wasn't afraid of her appetite. Being Italian, he grew up around food and women who loved to eat.

Throw all that in with what he knew of her from coming into the restaurant; dedicated, responsible, hard-working, and caring, and you had the perfect woman, not that he was destined for marriage.

After all, I am my father's son. That thought scared him away from the most casual relationship, and Kaylee deserved something more than that. She deserved what he would never be able to give her. He might give the façade well, like his father had. But eventually all masks come off, and Luciano would never risk hurting a woman the way his mom had been hurt. That's why he kept his distance from Kaylee. He refused to hurt her, and that's exactly what would happen.

Everything he had went into making *Luciano's* a success. The restaurant was the only mistress he had time for. Physically, he'd gotten what he wanted when he wanted it, except for the past six months. Since then, all he'd wanted was a certain, dark-skinned beauty that spilled more drinks than any woman he'd ever met, a woman he shouldn't want. The connection to what his brain knew, and his dick wanted, was severed and there didn't seem to be a thing to do about it.

Yeah, I think it's better I don't see her tonight. Maybe the extra break would do the big guy some good.

Why did this have to happen today?

A large shipment of books came in early which usually made her happy. Today, it pissed her off. Too much work, not enough time. Her eyes struggled to stay open from lack of sleep the night before. Kaylee's computer had crashed and it took what felt like days for a *Geek Squad* geek to come and fix it for her. The Daniels curse attacked in full effect messing with her love life. No, not love, her sex life.

The minute the digital clock in her cramped bookstore read 6:00 PM, Kaylee closed up shop, and made her way to her apartment above the store to get dressed for tonight.

Black panty hose, check.

Black dress, check.

Heels that sucked to walk in, check.

After dressing in her seduction clothes, Kaylee went into her bathroom and fixed her hair. Raising her arms, she captured half the braids up in a clip, while the rest hung free down her back. A light coat of makeup already graced her face. Time to go, she thought, but her feet wouldn't move.

Smoothing down the stretched, black dress that clung to her curves a bit too tight for comfort, Kaylee took a few deep calming breaths. *I can do this. I'm a sexy, confident, independent woman prepared for the hunt. And I will get the damn buck.*

Leaning against the outer wall of *Luciano's*, Kaylee tried to calm her queasy stomach. Reaching in her purse, she downed a couple of Tums tablets and hoped for speedy results. *Yeah, like Tums will help*. This was nerves, not heartburn. Shifting slightly against the brick wall behind her back, something caught on her panty hose. Groaning, Kaylee lifted her leg from the wall to check her hose even though she really didn't need to see her leg to know what happened.

"Shit! Of course I had to get a run in my panty hose. God forbid I don't screw something up."

A short, elderly woman happened to walk by as Kaylee fussed at herself, bending down to examine the run in her pantyhose.

"I wouldn't worry about that tiny little run, dear. I'd be more worried about your top half. When the light shines on you, you can see right through your black dress. A lady should never wear a white bra under a black dress." Then she turned and walked away leaving Kaylee stunned.

"Oh God, I'm getting fashion tips from a ninety year old grandma on the street corner!" In frustration, she tried to run her hand through her hair before remembering she had it up.

What the hell is wrong with me? I can't do this. She obviously had a hard enough time dressing herself, how could she expect to seduce Luciano?

Remembering what the old woman had said, Kaylee wrapped her arms around her chest and attempted to get away from *Luciano's* as fast as her cheap stilettos would carry her. Unfortunately, she hit a wall, a hard, muscular, oh so yummy smelling wall. Luciano.

As Kaylee's face lay smashed against Luciano's broad chest she couldn't bring herself to pull away. His rich, musky, scent mixed with sweet Italian herbs swirled around her causing a Luciano induced trance.

She felt his hand firmly clasped around her arm, probably making sure he caught her when she tried to mow him down, but succeeding more in making her dizzy with lust. Kaylee buried her face in his chest trying to take him in while she had the chance, inhaling as much of his scent as she could. His strong heartbeat pulsed against her cheek and she did the craziest thing. Nothing could hold her back. Kaylee took a deep, longing breath, and sighed. Right there, on the street, against his chest.

"Um, Kaylee? Is everything alright?" The sound of his voice was enough to bring her out of her trance enough so that shock set in.

Holy Mother of God. Am I really standing here smelling him?

Kaylee tried to bolt away from him as though he had electrocuted her. Yeah, she was singed all right. The wires in her brain were at least.

All because of Luciano.

Her attempt to pull away failed as he tightened his grip on her arm. It didn't hurt, but the hold was tight enough to keep her in place. She could do nothing except respond. *Maybe he didn't notice. Just act normal*.

"Fine...I mean yeah. I'm alright. How are you?"

Luciano reached out with his left hand twisting one of her braids with his finger. "You were sighing."

Think, think, think. With Luciano tucked against her body and his hand in her hair, thinking didn't come easy. "I was... clearing... my... throat?" she replied meekly.

"Clearing your throat, huh?" he smiled. "Sounded more like a sigh to me. Not that I'm complaining. I think it was pretty damn sexy."

Sexy? Did she hear him correctly? Did Luciano just say that something about her was sexy? Naw, she must have heard wrong.

"Nope. No sighing here. Like I said, I just had to clear my throat."

"That's a shame," Luciano twirled her hair tighter. "I think I would have preferred a sigh."

Kaylee's mind fogged over in a haze of confusion. She didn't have much experience; actually, she didn't have experience at all with a man like Luciano. If she didn't know better, she might think he was flirting with her.

Wishful thinking, girl. He isn't going to make your job that easy for you.

"Where were you going in such a hurry?" he asked.

"I was going to go change before I met the girls tonight. I had an um, job interview?" *Brilliant, Kaylee. Lie to the man*.

"I thought you owned your own bookstore."

Kaylee watched the easy smile spread across his face as he spoke.

"I did. I mean, I do. I was interviewing someone I might hire. I thought I should dress up too, you know, just to be professional."

"I see," Luciano told her. Then, still playing with the strand of hair in his fingers, he said, "Your hair looks different today. What did you do to it?"

Kaylee stood there, her eyes transfixed on his, unable to answer his question. She knew she should, but she couldn't, not with his hand in her hair this seductively.

Finally, she remembered her plan and tried to keep conversation going with him. "I call it chocolate cherry."

He stared at her "Call what chocolate cherry?"

You are such a ditz, Kaylee. "My hair. I had my braids redone and wanted to go for something different. I threw some red in and call it chocolate cherry. A girl can never get enough chocolate cherries."

Then two things struck Kaylee, neither of which she was proud of. First of all, she was rambling. She never rambled. She was the cool, calm and collected one; the dependable, stable one. But not around Luciano. Around Luciano she became either a mute, or a babbling ditz.

The second thing she noticed was she'd told him she picked hair colors from foods she like to eat. She didn't know much about flirting and seducing a man, but she did know you shouldn't tell them you are crazy enough to color your hair after a food.

"I like it," Luciano said snapping her out of her internal lecture. "Your outfit too. I don't see why you want to change."

The warm touch of Luciano's hand along with the complement had Kaylee ready to open her mouth and blurt out the fact that she wanted him. Here and now. But she didn't.

Kaylee glanced around and for the first time remembered they were on the sidewalk next to his restaurant. Pedestrians walked by them, cars drove by. No, the *here part* probably wasn't the best idea.

"Thanks, I really think I should go change though." *Or maybe you'd like to go with me and help me out of this dress?*

"I don't."

Luciano's voice was firm causing her heart to accelerate. Luciano obviously liked to be in control. Embarrassingly enough, that turned her on more than she wanted to admit, even to herself.

"Well, I wouldn't want to be late meeting Bri and Tabby." *Who gives a crap if I'm flashing the whole restaurant?* At that moment, Kaylee didn't care about anything. She only wanted to revel in the feel and succulent smell of Luciano. His masculine scent affected her like what spinach did to Popeye. It gave her strength. *Huh, maybe I can do this*, she thought. And almost let out another sigh. Or maybe she did.

Luciano knew he should walk away from Kaylee before he did something really stupid like kiss her full lips. *What the hell are you doing man? Get your hand out of her hair and back up.*

It was damn hard to do. The way her sexy, curvaceous body stood tucked against his own, the soft seductive sighs she made without her own knowledge, the silky feel of her hair. Yeah, it's time to get the hell out of dodge. Not to mention the fact that he needed to get back in the restaurant and finish fixing the dishwasher. What had he even come out for in the first place?

"I better get going," Luciano said. "I have to get a few tools from my car and get back in. We have a broken dishwasher I need to tend to."

"Oh, okay. It was good talking with you," she replied without backing away.

Luciano fought his own urges and backed away from Kaylee's warm, soft body. He memorized her black clad curves. The swell of her breasts peaked out above her dress. Creamy, brown skin beckoned him, begging him to rub his hands all over her. Damn she was hot.

As his eyes continued to take her in, Luciano noticed something he hadn't before. How did it skip his attention? The dress that wrapped around her body wasn't only hot, he could also see though it. Now he knew that behind her sexy little outfit she wore a white bra. He wanted more than just to know it, he wanted to see it. Badly. Looked like the big guy wouldn't be getting a break tonight. He already gave Kaylee his full attention.

As much as her body begged to be touched, her mouth begged to be kissed. Suffering from brief insanity, he almost did it. Then he glanced into the nervous look in her honey brown eyes and reality set in.

Kaylee would want a relationship. Kaylee wasn't the 'have a little fun and leave everything behind' type of woman. And that's exactly the type of woman he needed. Whether he liked it or not. Right now, he didn't like it one bit. At least a certain part of him didn't like it. He wanted to be buried inside her for a very long time. A no end in sight kind of long.

"Good night," Luciano knew he said the words abruptly but figured it for the best. He then turned and walked towards his black car. He felt Kaylee's eyes on his back as he went and damned if he didn't want to go back to her and run his hands through her silky hair one more time, but he didn't.

Luciano lingered at his car before grabbing his tools and heading back into his restaurant. He needed to avoid seeing Kaylee again. She most likely had already made her way into the restaurant but he didn't want to take any chances at seeing her again tonight. For some reason he was off his game and the desire to have her became more desperate, more urgent.

A few minutes later, his hands deep within the motor of the dishwasher, Luciano thought about Kaylee. He didn't know what drew him to her, but it was fierce, something he never experienced before.

Pushing his hair back as it fell in his face, he bent to remove a screw from the dishwasher. The sounds of pans clanking, hurried feet across the tile floor, and anxious voices swirled around him. He needed to keep his head clear and focus on *Luciano's*. The restaurant was his life and he needed to make it a success. He didn't have time in his life to get involved with a woman like Kaylee.

Just keep reminding yourself of that.

The moment Kaylee walked into Luciano's the queasy feeling was back in the pit of her stomach. How was she supposed to act around Luciano tonight? She struggled enough with him on a regular basis. Now, after the way he touched her this evening, and the way he abruptly stalked away, she really didn't know how to approach him.

In reality, she should have gone for it on the sidewalk, flirted a bit and maybe even tried to kiss him. Fear stopped her. She may have passed up her very best chance. Would she have another chance like that one? If she did, would she be brave enough to snatch it? *This seducing business is tough stuff.*

Kaylee smiled at the familiar surroundings she had grown to love. The sweet and tangy smell of tomato sauce and garlic filled the air causing a growl to form in the pit of her stomach.

"Is your gorgeous friend coming tonight?"

At the sound of Nico's voice she became startled and almost tripped. It was almost another Kaylee screws up moment. At least this time Luciano wouldn't be present.

"She always comes with me, doesn't she?" her irritation at herself coming out at Nico. She wanted Nico to be Luciano so she'd have another chance. She knew she'd royally screwed up outside by not taking action.

"Just making sure. Tonight is my night to win her over. I can feel it." Nico studied Kaylee before asking, "Are you cold?"

"I wouldn't hold your breath, Nico. She seems to be immune to your charm," she teased.

Leaning down close to her ear to speak, he said, "No woman is immune to me, sweetheart. Some of them just take a little longer to come around." He then turned and walked towards the kitchen.

Kaylee headed to the table that they held for them every Friday night, weaving through the other round tables and chuckling softly. She liked Nico, but he spelled trouble for Tabby. He was a compulsive flirt and she was a woman hungry for love. They would mix like oil and water. She hoped Tabby continued to have the sense to realize it. So far, she had.

Kaylee enjoyed talking with him. *I wonder why I can't talk with Luciano as easily as I can Nico? Because you don't want Nico, and you want, Luciano.* It made a whole different ball game.

Wiping her clammy palms on her dress Kaylee sat down and scanned the room for Luciano. She didn't see him anywhere. Go figure. She reached out and downed a glass of water. Still no Luciano. Glancing at her watch, she realized it was 7:25. Had she really wasted that much time outside? It felt like seconds. Where the heck did Luciano go?

The dishwasher. He said something about fixing a dishwasher. With her luck, she wouldn't get the chance to see him the rest of the night. Here she was ready to release her inner sex kitten and her target was nowhere to be seen. Looks like the Daniels' curse struck again.

Chapter Three

Brianna and Tabby walked in a couple of minutes later.

"Did you talk to him? I bet it was so romantic," Tabby said the second she sat down at the table.

"Nope," Kaylee replied before taking her apple martini straight from the hand of her waiter to take a swig.

"Why the hell not, girl? You chicken out?" Bri asked.

"No I didn't chicken out. I kind of forgot what I should be doing."

"You what?" both her friends said in unison, confusion in their faces.

"Well I couldn't help it." Kaylee tried to lower her voice so no one else could hear. "He had his hands in my hair, I kept sighing, and I think he called me sexy. How do you expect me to remember anything under those conditions?"

"I think I missed a step here," Bri said.

"You and me both," Tabby added.

They took the words from Kaylee's mouth. She'd been there but somehow missed a step along the way as well. After downing another drink, Kaylee went through the whole story; from the nosy old lady, to almost trampling Luciano, and finally ending with the touching and sighing. Both girls listened and watched. Anticipation marked their faces while Kaylee spilled the whole tale.

"Let me get this straight. He told you he liked your hair, which does look good by the way," Bri added her opinion. "He wrapped your braids around his finger, and told you you were sexy and you did nothing?" Brianna asked in disbelief.

"I couldn't think. By the time I thought about it he was leaving and I haven't seen him since."

Brianna grabbed the waiter's attention and ordered another round of apple martinis, breaking their one martini rule. "I can't believe you let him go."

"Give her a little break, Bri," Tabby said standing up for Kaylee. "She's trying. It isn't easy to approach a man and tell him you want to have your way with him. I've been through the ringer on my quest to find Mr. Right."

"Especially when he's the Italian Stud," Bri laughed.

"Back up a minute there, girl," Kaylee exclaimed. "I don't want Mr. Right. I want to add a little bit of excitement to my life, a fling, that's it. I'm too busy with *Bookends* to concentrate on a relationship."

"Whatever you say, Kay." Tabby didn't get it.

"Hey, ladies. How ya doing?" Nico said approaching their table, plates in hand.

It was Tabby who replied. "We're okay. Where's Luciano tonight?" The last word came out broken due to Kaylee's reflexes causing her foot to connect with Tabby's shin.

"He's back there having a fit over the busted dishwasher. I can't stay out here with you guys tonight. I just wanted to bring your Parmesan Chicken out to you and see Tabby's beautiful face," he said winking at her.

"I give you an 'A' for effort, Nico. You don't give up do you?" Bri asked.

"No. I always win. Might as well give up now, Tabby. You will be mine." Then just as quickly as he approached the table, he was gone.

"Is there some unwritten rule that they both have to get us all flustered and then walk their fine asses away?" Kaylee asked as the martinis started to go to her head.

"I think you're the only one that gets flustered, Kay," Tabby said. "I don't want Nico the way you want Luciano."

"You're crazy then," Bri said laughing. "That man has it going on. He'd be a great lay."

"Shh," Kaylee shushed her while Tabby sat across the table staring at the closed kitchen doors. "You are so bad, Bri."

"Someone in this group has to be. There's no one else to do it since the two of you are wound up so tight," Bri laughed.

Kaylee smiled at her friend. *Bri loved to stir the pot.*

"Well, I guess I better have a few more drinks and loosen up," Kaylee said tilting her glass up to take a swallow.

The three ladies closed the restaurant that night. One drink after another lead to a martini drinking contest that took awhile. They drank, laughed and talked. By the time *Luciano's* closed they had all drank too much to drive, so after calling for cabs they stumbled from the restaurant giggling like schoolgirls.

"I don't feel so good, guys," Brianna leaned against the wall outside. She didn't look good either. Her dark skin started fading to a pale brown.

"Since the two of us live so close to one another, maybe I should ride with her," Tabby offered.

"Yeah, maybe you should." Kaylee agreed worried about her friend.

About that time the first cab pulled up while Brianna started to look sicker by the minute.

"Go ahead and take the first one. I think she needs to get home." The fresh air felt good against Kaylee's skin. Might as well let Tab get Bri home since she didn't mind the wait.

"Are you sure you'll be okay out here by yourself?" Tabby asked.

Kaylee could tell her friend didn't want to leave her by herself.

"Yeah, I'll be fine. My cab should come any minute." Kaylee waved them away.

"Thanks, Kay," Bri mumbled as she made her way into the cab with Tabby not far behind her.

"Your woman looked hot tonight, boss," Nico said to Luciano as they prepared to leave the restaurant for the night.

With a frustrated groan, Luciano said, "First of all, she isn't my woman. Second, how many times do I have to tell you to quit calling me boss?"

"If she isn't your woman, why'd you know exactly who I was talking about?" Nico replied smugly.

Fuck. I blew that one. "Because I know you bone head. You always have something to say about Kaylee."

Luciano knew the reason for that, his cousin knew him a lot better than he wanted to admit. They'd always been more like brothers than cousins.

"I see the way you look at her. If she's not your woman yet she will be." Nico headed towards the kitchen to dispose of some towels before coming out to see Luciano again. "You want her. I don't know why you don't go for it. It might do you some good to get laid."

"I have no problem getting laid and I think it might do you some good to mind your own business," Luciano said hotly.

"Testy, aren't we tonight?"

Sometimes Nico drove him crazy, but he couldn't help but laugh. He had a way about him, outgoing and carefree, much different than his own personality.

"I've had a long night, Nic. Get your shit and let's get out of here."

Luciano stood by the door waiting for Nico. Why couldn't he get Kaylee out of his mind? This lust thing he had going really fuckin' sucked. Why his dick picked her to become fixated on, he didn't know. Okay, maybe he did know why, but that didn't make things any easier to deal with.

He found it damn hard to concentrate with a hard-on every Friday night. He had lack of blood flowing to his head the second she walked into the room—well, lack of blood flow to the head on top of his neck. The lower one didn't lack that in the least.

Luciano looked around the restaurant trying to regain his focus. *This is what's important*, he told himself. This is what he was meant for, restaurant owner, not boyfriend. *You're just like your father*. The words echoed in his head before he shook them out. Temporarily.

Nico joined Luciano at the door and they both headed out, Luciano turned to lock the door as they went.

Stepping out onto the sidewalk, a cool breeze brushed across his body bringing with it the scent of warm vanilla. Now he was starting to smell her when she wasn't around. Not a good sign.

"I'm glad this night is finally over," Luciano said to his cousin. "I thought it would never end."

"I know how you can unwind." Nico pointed toward the outer wall of the restaurant.

There, on the San Francisco street corner, stood Kaylee, looking just as beautiful as she had earlier. Under the light, he again noticed the white of her alluring bra. Temptation snapped at him. A hunger for what he knew she would be able to give him.

"Fuck." Luciano ran his hand through his black hair. "What the hell is she doing out here at night by herself?"

"Only one way to find out," Nico taunted him.

Luciano stood there watching her lean against the wall, quickly glancing at her watch. "Go ahead and head home, Nic. I'll go make sure she's okay."

"I'm sure you will, boss," Nico replied with a wink.

Luciano let the boss comment slide. "I'm just going to see if she needs a ride."

"And what kind of ride would that be?"

Luciano watched as Nico's expression sobered. Obviously he realized Luciano didn't consider his joke the least bit funny.

"Just a joke, boss. Take a deep breath and relax." Nico patted Luciano on the back. "Now go get her." He walked away in the opposite direction.

Temptation would be hard to avoid tonight.

What's taking this cab so long? Kaylee wondered leaning against the same brick wall from earlier. Her thoughts traveled to what transpired earlier with Luciano. It felt like a lifetime ago, *must be the alcohol* she thought. She usually stuck to one martini a night. Tonight, she ended at five.

The alcohol must have done her some good. At this moment, she felt wild and free, totally able to seduce the Italian Stud. Would she ever be lucky enough to experience Luciano first hand? Seducing him would be hard, but she wanted him so bad it made everything worth it.

A slight wind brushed against her skin and she imagined the breeze as Luciano's hands, the sensation, almost too much to handle. "See what drinking does to you?" she asked herself. She was already wet standing outside a restaurant just thinking about the owner.

Trying to turn off her over-active imagination, Kaylee distracted herself by reaching into her purse for a breath mint. Suddenly footsteps heading towards her were a whole new distraction. Kaylee already knew exactly who it would be.

This is it, Kaylee. God finally smiled down on her tonight by sending Luciano her way, offering her a second chance. Feeling last minute jitters, her hands fidgeted with the mint box, trying to close if before stuffing in the little black purse that hung on her shoulder. The alcohol probably didn't help the situation. Her motor skills now had two reasons to act up. This might be easier if she wasn't drunk, but hey, it might dull the rejection if he turned her down.

"What are you doing out here by yourself at this time of night, Kaylee?"

He stood before her, masculinity personified, and she went mute, couldn't think of a thing to say. Opening her mouth she made a half-hearted attempt before closing it. How would she ever be able to tell this gorgeous man she wanted him? Supposedly alcohol loosened some people up. Apparently it had the opposite effect on Kaylee.

Luciano had her in a trance. His midnight eyes hypnotizing her and there wasn't a darn thing she could do about it. She wasn't all that sure she wanted to do anything about it either. Staring into his eyes wouldn't be a bad way to spend the next week.

"Are you okay? Do you need to sit down?" Luciano asked as he reached out his hand and grabbed her arm.

"Yes. I mean no. Well, yes, I'm okay and no, I don't need to sit down," she said in a hurried tone, but at least she'd found her voice.

Luciano let go of her arm. The limb immediately ached for his touch.

"Why are you out here alone? Where did your friends go?"

He made her dizzy with all his questions or maybe his eyes were doing that too.

"They took a cab; I'm waiting for mine to arrive." *Please don't come right now Mr. Cab driver.* Funny how she wished just the opposite not five minutes before.

"They shouldn't have left you out here alone, Bella." Luciano's hand reached up and stroked her cheek. "Come with me. I'll take you home."

Who the hell is Bella? She'd had a bit too much to drink but she was pretty sure her name wasn't Bella. Kaylee, that sounded more like it. Wow, the martinis went to her head quickly all of a sudden. "No. You don't have to do that," Kaylee said remembering he'd offered her a ride to her apartment. Where her bed was. *What are you saying Kaylee? Of course you want the man to take you home. How else will you be able to seduce him?*

"I insist. My car's this way."

Turning to the left, Luciano grabbed her arm in a gentle, but firm enough grasp that told her he wouldn't take no for an answer. Excitement surged through her body at his persistence.

Walking towards Luciano's car sounded much easier than reality proved. Her legs wobbled beneath her and her feet wanted to stumble. Somehow able to keep her gait steady, Kaylee walked as closely to Luciano as possible, his warm body taking away the nip in the air. Inhaling she savored the smell of his spicy, sweet scent. The scent was a contradiction, but somehow, uniquely Luciano. His intoxicating smell didn't come from a bottle, but the man himself.

Did the martinis or the man cause her brain to feel slightly fogged, and her legs to feel weak? A toss up, she decided.

"Why are you so intent on taking me home?"

"You're a woman waiting alone for a cab at night. My mama would never forgive me if I left you here."

Not quite the answer she wanted to hear. She'd hoped for something along the lines of, "You're so hot I can't keep my hands off you any longer." But no, she gets the whole my mama would never forgive me speech. "Oh. I see. Well, I don't live far."

Luciano continued to lead her to his black Mercedes and opened the passenger door for her. Such the gentlemen, he helped her inside before letting go of her arm and closing the door behind her. Her skin felt cold in the wake of his touch.

Luciano got into the car, and inserted the key. Kaylee listened as the car smoothly purred to life. Everything about him seemed to be smooth, the way he spoke, his fluid movement, and even his damn car. *I'm so out of my league. But I don't even give a damn.*

At the same time that thought flowed through her head, she watched in anticipation as Luciano began to move towards her, his hand reaching out. What would he do? Would he kiss her? Touch her?

Would her goal really be this easy to achieve.

"You almost forgot your seatbelt," he said as he reached out, grabbed the belt, and locked it into place.

Damn. Of course it wouldn't be that easy.

How do you seduce a man when you don't even know if he wants you or not? To seduce or not to seduce? That is the question. Maybe the bigger question should be, is he even on the market to be seduced. She knew he wasn't married, but he could be in a relationship. She knew plenty of women wanted him. She overheard a few arguments on her Friday nights when jealous husbands and boyfriends noticed their women ogling him.

"Which way should I go?" he asked breaking the silence.

Kaylee pointed Luciano in the right direction and the silence resumed for the next few minutes. They only spoke enough to offer or receive driving directions. As he drove his car hit several potholes. The bumpy, sharp movements of the car caused her to become nauseated. The longer she rode in the car, the more her inebriation became obvious.

Deciding to try and get her mind off her woozy stomach and back onto Luciano, Kaylee started conversation.

"Tell me a little bit about yourself." *Huh. Not too bad.*

"What would you like to know?"

Okay. So he wasn't going to make this easy. She glanced over to see Luciano gripping the steering wheel tightly. Did he regret offering her a ride? Did he not want to answer her? Questions bombarded her already alcohol induced foggy brain.

"Are you umm… dating anyone? You know, just out of curiosity."

Luciano made eye contact with her. Instantly mesmerized, a familiar ache formed at the juncture of her thighs.

A half smile tugged at the corner of his mouth as he said to her, "That's an interesting question."

Heat flooded Kaylee's cheeks. "I'm sorry."

"Don't be." His tension visually eased. "I'm unattached. I like it that way. What about you?"

Her head couldn't take much more confusion in its current state. Her emotions flip flopping like a fish out of water. Disappointment came over her when he said he liked being single. That sounded like a hint. But then she could be reading too much into his comment. She was known to do that from time to time, and he did ask about her relationship status. That had to count for something, right?

"Do I get an answer?" Luciano chuckled.

"I'm single." In case Luciano was as easily confused as she seemed to be, Kaylee didn't tack on the fact that she liked being single as well.

"Good to know, Bella. I hate to change the subject but I thought you said you didn't live far." Luciano turned briefly as he spoke to her.

Kaylee glanced around her looking at the street names, and numbers. Embarrassed beyond belief she could only muster up two words. "I don't," before she buried her face in her hands.

"And I thought you were finally warming up to me," Luciano kidded. "Are we back to one and two word phrases, Kaylee? I don't bite you know. Not unless I'm asked at least."

That sounded nice. He'd probably take it back after he realized he said it to a complete ding bat.

"Luciano?"

"Yeah."

She thought she felt close to puking before, now she had to physically fight back the urge. "You have to turn around. I live about three miles back."

A few minutes later, Luciano pulled up to the curb and killed the engine, but said nothing.

Man, did she blow it? He probably thought she was a head case; a twenty eight year old woman who consistently spilled beverages, had trouble speaking, and who couldn't even remember where she lived.

"Well, thanks for the ride," she finally managed to say.

"You live in your bookstore?"

"Just about," she replied. "I live in an apartment on top, but the majority of my time is spent in the store."

"You sound like me. I'd love an apartment above *Luciano's*."

This was the most natural conversation they'd ever had and she hated to see it end, but the longer she sat in the car, the more she realized she needed fresh air before she did something that really embarrassed her.

"Thanks again for the ride. I need to get in. I have to be at work at 10:00 tomorrow morning."

"Hang tight. I'll get the door and walk you to your apartment."

"You don't have to." As soon has the words left her mouth, she prayed for a do-over.

Luciano lifted his hand and placed a finger to her lips. "Shh. I want to."

"Okay," Kaylee replied in a hushed voice, fighting the urge to lick his finger, maybe even draw it into her mouth for a sensuous suck. *Snap out of it, Kaylee. Hold off a few more minutes.*

Kaylee lead the way to her apartment with Luciano by her side. His fluid, smooth, movements the opposite of her rushed ones. They approached the concrete steps that lead up to her second floor home, the black railing helped tremendously to keep her steady on her feet.

Flipping through her purse at the top of the stairs, Kaylee dug out her set of keys, making a movement towards the door.

"Here, let me do that for you." Luciano took the keys and inserted it into the lock.

Martini god give me strength. Grabbing his hand, Kaylee turned Luciano to face her. *Now or never,* she thought. Rising up onto her tiptoes, Kaylee lightly planted her lips on his, kissing him softly.

Finally! Luciano took the kiss a step further, coaxing her lips open, exploring the depths of her mouth. Kaylee did the same, her tongue starting out timidly before plunging into the warmth of his mouth. He tasted better than Belgian chocolate, felt better than the sunshine on her skin, and smelled like hot, sexy man.

The warm, inviting, contours of his mouth welcomed her, eased her nervousness. His tongue danced with hers in a quick trip around the dance floor before he pulled away.

"I'm sorry. I shouldn't have kissed you. I thought...I mean...I wanted...oh hell, I don't know." Kaylee grabbed her door handle, twisted the knob, and ran smack dab into her front door.

The Daniels' Curse.

"Shit!" She cursed out of embarrassment and sadness. Fighting back tears, she held her nose, hoping it wasn't swollen. Not even the Martini god dulled the pain of this rejection.

The way he initially opened up to her, taking her in, and caressing her tongue with his own, Kaylee thought herself home free. Thought just maybe, he wanted her too.

Struggling to turn the key she'd foolishly pulled from him earlier, she fought to shield her face from his view.

"Here, let me help you."

"No thanks, I'm fine," she replied in a sarcastic tone. "I appreciate the ride. Good night."

"Wait, Bella," Luciano commanded, preventing her from opening the door. "We need to talk."

"What is there to talk about?" she wanted to know. "Do you want to rehash the fact that I made a fool of myself? Or the fact that I've been turned down by the man I've been lusting after for six months. Or even better, we can talk about the fact that I preceded to run into a door after I kissed said man. Which is it?"

Her mama's temper emerged in full force. But she couldn't help it. All she'd held in wanted free. At the same time, a blanket of embarrassment came over her. Had she really just admitted to lusting after him? Tears stung her eyes.

"Bella, if you'll calm down for just a second we can talk this out."

The name made her pause a minute before she remembered he'd used it before. Whoever this Bella person was, she'd just made Kaylee's night a whole lot worse. A girl never wanted a man to call her by a different name after she kissed him.

"We don't have anything to talk about. I think I understand completely."

Luciano ran his hand through his coal-black hair. "Did you have to take the cab because you had been drinking?" Then more to himself than her he said, "I should have realized you had been drinking when you didn't drive your car home."

"I don't see what that has to do with anything, but yes. I don't drink and drive. I'm trying to liven my life up a bit but not get myself killed."

"You don't have to make excuses for not driving while intoxicated. I respect that. I just want to know how you plan to get your car tomorrow. Maybe we can meet up and talk then."

Shaking her head vehemently, Kaylee said, "Thanks, but no thanks. My mama didn't raise no fool. I've had enough embarrassment to last a lifetime. I'll get up early to get my car before *Luciano's* opens."

She suddenly felt extremely dizzy.

"Good night." Kaylee walked into her apartment, locked the door, and stumbled into her bedroom to try and forget this night ever happened.

Chapter Four

Luciano didn't know why he set his alarm clock for 7:00 AM in hopes of catching Kaylee before she left her apartment, but he had. Sleep evaded him until the wee hours of the morning. He couldn't handle Kaylee thinking he didn't want her when that couldn't be any farther from the truth. Truth be told, he wanted her too much, not that she needed to know that. Mid tossing and turning, Luciano rolled over and set his alarm. Now here he was getting ready to leave the house to plead his case to a very pissed off Kaylee. To tell her he wanted her. That he'd wanted her last night.

She didn't realize how badly he wanted to take her, right there at her front door if she would let him. The out-of-control lust he felt for her almost made him do something he'd regret. She'd regret. Kaylee deserved to be taken slowly and passionately, not up against her front door in the heat of the moment.

Her taste still lingered in his mouth despite the time between their brief kiss and now. She tasted sweet and full of passion, a passion that in his sleepless night he'd decided he had to experience again. Letting Kaylee go without having her would be a mistake of gigantic proportions. He wanted her. She wanted him. It was chemistry. Who was he to fight science?

His mind still reeled over what she said the night before. She planned to try and liven up her life? Yeah, he could help with that. They'd have a damn good time in the process too.

Luciano fidgeted in the seat of his car trying to get comfortable. Damn she had him on the edge of a cliff. And he planned to jump off. After he secured his parachute by talking with her. Then maybe the hold the sweet and shy Kaylee had on him would be released.

"Sweet and shy my ass," Luciano said as he drove into the drive-thru donut shop. She hadn't been sweet and shy when she thought he had rejected her. No, no. Kaylee could be a pistol if she felt threatened. Last night she had been pissed, opinionated, and sexy as hell.

"Excuse me sir, are you ready to order?"

"Sorry," Luciano mumbled realizing he'd ignored the woman try-ing to take his order. "I'll take two large coffees, cream and sugar, and a dozen mixed donuts."

Not knowing what Kaylee liked, he ordered as much as possible. "Make sure you don't put cream and sugar in the coffee. Just a few packets in the bag," he amended.

For some reason, Luciano didn't want to admit, he wanted this morning to go perfectly. He had the feeling he'd need all the help he could get. If she greeted him the way she dismissed him last night, it would be one hell of a fight, but one he intended to win.

Kaylee awoke to someone pounding on her head.

What the hell?

Boom, boom, boom. The pounding returned, this time, coming from her living room.

The front door, not her head, had someone pounding away like crazy. That made more sense. Lying in her bed, Kaylee hoped whoev-er dared wake her this early after a night of drinking would go away. Images began popping in her head but they were all fuzzy and didn't make a clear picture.

They all circled around Luciano. She quickly decided she must have been dreaming about him again last night. Nothing new there. Closing her eyes, Kaylee rolled over forgetting the misplaced images in her head.

Boom, boom, boom. Whoever was banging on her door wasn't going away. She glanced at the clock which read, 7:45. No way would Bri or Tab be at her door, especially after the night they had at *Luciano's*. Who could it be?

Kaylee dragged her weary body from bed, stretched, and scratched a tickle on her nose.

"Ouch," she cried out. The pain brought back the memories of the night before. Disappointment, drinking... Luciano. A slide show began to flash through her mind, Luciano taking her home, passing her house, kissing him, then, the mother of all nightmares, running into the door.

Damn alcohol. How could she have kissed Luciano and then done something as idiotic as running into the door? Why did she drink last night of all nights?

Another bang pierced through her head. Angry at herself she stormed into her living room ready to ream whoever had come over this early. She readied herself and opened the door to none other than Luciano himself.

Luciano took in the sight of the just rolled out of bed version of Kaylee. It wasn't quite the way he wanted the first time he saw her like this to be, but it still tasted sweet.

Her long, shiny hair still looked gorgeous. Her eyes were puffy from lack of sleep, her lips still as sexy as ever, and her nose, slightly swollen on the end. She must have hit it harder than he realized.

Out of nowhere the urge came to kiss the end of her nose. But he couldn't. Not right now, not with that scowl on her face.

Wandering eyes moved from her face to her choice of bedtime apparel. She wore an over-sized, red, shirt that said, "Don't talk to me until I've had my coffee." Thank God he brought some. The damn thing came clear down to her knees yet his body began to react immediately. She consistently had this effect on him. He needed a few nights with her to get her out of his system. That's all, just a few nights.

"A peace offering." Luciano raised the paper cup of hot coffee hoping to God she'd let him in. She did. First, taking the piping hot cup of coffee from his hands and then stepping aside for him to enter before she headed straight for the kitchen.

Luciano handed her the cream and sugar before taking himself and the donuts into Kaylee's living room. Her apartment was homey, clean, with everything in its proper place. You could tell a lot from a person by their home and what he saw of Kaylee's fit her to a tee.

A small dark green love seat sat against the back wall. On the opposite wall was a small TV on a dark wood table with her VCR and DVD player below.

She had another wood table that matched the one her TV set was on that was between the couch and a matching recliner chair. When Luciano turned his attention to the far wall he saw what he knew to be Kaylee's passion, books. There were two large bookshelves packed with different books. He stepped forward and noticed they were all grouped together by authors in alphabetical order.

His little perfectionist. No, she wasn't his and she never would be. He'd better remember that. He wanted to bury himself in that luscious body for hours, but she wasn't his.

Luciano sat down on her couch and waited for Kaylee to join him. Seconds later he again had the chance to see her cute little outfit when she came over and sat on the chair, sipping her coffee. Neither of them spoke.

Finally, Kaylee broke the silence by asking, "Care to tell me why you're here?"

"I'm trying to let you drink your coffee first." He pointed to her shirt. "I figured I needed all the help I could get so you'd forgive me for last night."

He watched her lips form a frown. Damn the woman was cute when mad. He could practically see the wheels turning in her head, trying to think of an excuse for the night before.

She failed.

"I don't know what you're talking about," she tried to lie while running her hand through her hair before continuing, "I don't remember a thing. You make awfully strong martinis."

Luciano tried to hide his amusement, which he noticed he did a lot around her. She fascinated him on many levels and that wasn't an easy feat. But Kaylee managed it with ease. She probably didn't even realize she did it. That made her all the more interesting.

"I'm feeling a bit insulted. If my kiss was that forgettable, I have some work to do," he smiled.

"Well I'm sorry to insult Sir Luciano the Italian Stud!" she said in a raised voice.

Luciano laughed heartily. "Italian Stud, huh? Where'd you get that one?" His laughter suddenly ceased as he looked over and noticed her angry scowl turned into something altogether different. The creamy dark skin began to pale faster by the second.

"I think I'm going to be sick." Kaylee set her coffee down and ran for what he assumed was the bathroom.

Kaylee made it to the bathroom just in time. Her stomach had been uneasy due to her night but after she spouted the Italian Stud comment, it became much, much worse.

Even worse, she began to think herself crazy. Why did this man unnerve her so much? Why did she always say the wrong thing or do the wrong thing, or plain embarrass herself in his company? It wasn't like her to be this way. It pissed her off that she couldn't control herself around him.

Just freaking perfect. What made him even come over? She was unprepared; not that being prepared usually helped her when it concerned Luciano.

Luciano knocked softly on the door. "You okay in there?"

He sounded concerned which embarrassed her all the more. "Fine," she called back. "Just wishing I could flush myself down the toilet, too."

"I would really rather you not flush yourself down the toilet. At least not until after we finish our talk."

She couldn't help but laugh. Despite one catastrophe after the other, she still wanted him. Still, today her emotions were out of whack. She'd gone from embarrassed, to mad, to embarrassed again, to puking.

No, today wasn't the day to put her plan into action.

"I'm still a little woozy in here. Why don't you go on home? I'll call Tabby to drive me over to get my car later."

"Nice try," Luciano said slowly opening the door. "We aren't done yet."

"Umm. You're getting a little personal here don't you think? I just finished worshiping the porcelain god and I'm a mess."

Luciano opened her linen closet and pulled out a washcloth. He then amazed her even more by wetting the cloth, and bending down to brush it across her forehead.

"What…What are you doing?" Could this really be happening? If it happened to be a dream, Kaylee didn't want to wake up. She wanted to savor the unfamiliar feel of being pampered.

"I'm wiping the sweat off your forehead," he said matter-of-factly.

"Why?" Utter confusion filled her mind. Why would he do his for her?

"My mama raised me as a gentleman."

Kaylee looked up at Luciano. "She must be a wonderful woman."

"She is."

She sensed a great sadness in him, his dark eyes becoming more distant as he stroked her forehead.

"I didn't mean to say that," Kaylee said out of the blue.

"Say what, Bella?"

"The Italian Stud comment. It slipped. Bri called you by that name. I don't usually yell at people, so I didn't know what else to say."

Luciano stood and pulled Kaylee to her feet. "While I don't go around thinking of myself as a stud, I kind of like the idea that you do." He still held her onto her. "And you yelled at me last night, too. I think you do a pretty good job with it."

Was it her he liked to think of him as a stud, or women in general? She itched to ask but held her tongue. "I guess there's just something about you that drives me crazy." In more ways than one she wanted to say, but couldn't bring herself to do it.

"I'm glad you brought that up because you drive me crazy too."

"I do?" Kaylee knew her voice came out timid and unsure, but at this moment, she didn't care. Her body began to buzz to life. He had to mean that in the way she thought he did.

She felt Luciano's grip on her hand tighten. "There has to be a better place to do this than the bathroom," he told her. "Do whatever you need to do in here and I'll meet you in the living room."

Kaylee watched as he turned and headed for the other room. For a quick moment she feared she might get sick again. Her nerves were completely shot and her mind struggled to figure out what Luciano would say to her. *I drive him crazy!* That excited her. She couldn't wait to find out what he planned to do about it. Maybe this seduction business wasn't so hard after all.

Quickly she grabbed her bright yellow toothbrush and brushed her teeth. After the way she spent the past few minutes, she knew her breath passed over the typical morning breath category and teetered on dangerous. Then re-wetting the cloth Luciano used on her earlier, she washed her face before tying her hair into a knot on the back of her head.

Briefly she considered going into her bedroom to change but scratched the idea. Whatever got into Luciano to make him come over, might not last long. She didn't want to risk the chance that he would be gone by the time she returned. Picking up her bottle of vanilla perfume she gave herself a quick spray. Plus, today just might be the morning to seduce him. The fewer clothes she had on, the better, right?

Taking one last glance in the mirror, and discovering she'd taken one small step up from just rolled out of bed, to rolled out of bed a little while ago, but *I'm too lazy to do anything with myself,* she walked out of the bathroom and down the hall towards Luciano. This was on her terms. She was in control.

Kaylee sat down on the chair she left vacated and waited for Luciano to talk to her. What did he have to say?

"First, I don't want you to be embarrassed for what you admitted to me last night," he started off by saying. "I've struggled with my attraction to you for some time now so there's no reason for you to be embarrassed about it."

Kaylee sat there trying to be cool.

"I'm tired of fighting it. If it hadn't been for the fact that you'd been drinking last night, I think we both would have ended the night very satisfied."

God she wanted to be satisfied by Luciano. Her body tingled at the thought. "Um. What did you just say?" She had to ask, couldn't help herself. Maybe someone slipped something in her drink last night and she was having some weird delayed reaction or something.

"You heard me right."

"So, that's the reason you pulled away last night?" First she had to know the answer to this question. She burned with the need.

"Yeah, that's why I pulled away last night. But in all honesty, I'm glad I did."

Of course, there had to be a but. *Should have known.* It couldn't be this easy. Not for Kaylee.

"Let me rephrase that. I still want you. I wanted you last night and I want you today. But it shouldn't have been the way it would have been last night."

Kaylee felt like jumping up and down screaming after he confirmed he wanted her. *He wants me. He wants me*, but she forced herself to remain cool.

"So you really want me?"

"Yes, I want you. You're beautiful. You have a body I've been dying to get my hands on, luscious and curvy. And you're fun, you make me laugh" Luciano winked at her, "you keep me on my toes."

Kaylee looked up at Luciano. "Holy shit," Her voice came out barley a whisper but she knew he heard her all the same.

"I tried to tell you last night but you wouldn't hear it. In fact, you yelled at me for doing something I consider pretty damn noble."

Her mind swirled. Luciano wanted her, that much she finally began to understand. But he did mention something about it not being the way it would have been last night. Was it just the alcohol or was she missing something else? Nothing ever came this easily for her. There had to be some kind of catch.

"You said things shouldn't have been the way they would have been last night. Is there more than just the drinking?" Luciano exhaled a deep, strong breath sending shivers down her arms.

"You need to know something. All I have to offer you is sex. Nothing more."

His voice held a strong, firm tone making her want to climb on his lap and take him right there. "Okay."

"I'm serious. I don't do relationships, Kaylee. I hate to sound harsh, but I need you to know that right up front. I don't want to pull any surprises on you. Before we decide if this goes any further I have to know you understand that."

Kaylee sat in her chair confused about all the talk of relationships. Where did it come from? The air around them held a tenseness that hadn't been there moments before. "Did I say something that makes you think I'm looking for a relationship with you?" After puking and everything else she managed to do in front of Luciano recently, talking was starting to come easier than it used to.

"You don't have to. I know the difference between a woman who just enjoys having a good time and women who want something more."

Something in his tone told Kaylee he believed her to be the latter. He had an arrogant streak she hadn't noticed before. She liked it, even though his assessment of her couldn't be farther off target.

"Listen, Luciano," Kaylee crossed her legs. "I'm going to put myself out here for a minute. I'm not looking for love or a relationship either. What I'm looking to do is add a little excitement to my life. I'm looking for the same thing you are—sex. I can't even guarantee how much time I'll have for that."

"Just sex," he repeated.

Kaylee saw the confused look on his face and continued, "I always do what's expected of me, and I'm looking to change that. With you. Like I told you last night, my plan was to seduce you."

Bri would be proud of her. Never before had she been this open and honest.

Kaylee waited for a reply. Luciano stared at her and she at him, neither speaking. Did she go overboard? Say too much? Scare him off? Somehow, she didn't think the Italian Stud would scare that easily. He seemed shocked but in a way that made her bubble with confidence. Kaylee tried to hide her smile.

"Do we have a deal?" Her inner Brianna attacked in full effect.

"We have a deal, Bella. I'll pick you up Monday night at seven for dinner."

"Dinner? I don't know if I can be ready that early on Monday. I usually work late everyday except for Friday," half of her didn't want to argue about this with him, but the other half wouldn't sacrifice her store just to get some.

"What time does your store close?"

"Six, but I still have stuff to do after closing time."

"Can you be ready by eight?"

If this was just about sex why was he so intent on taking her out to dinner? "Can't we just skip the dinner?" she asked.

"Damn woman. Don't say things like that to me. I'm already on a hair trigger here. I'm taking you out to dinner, so let's leave it at that. Can you be ready or not?" His voice was firm and tense.

"Yeah, I can be ready by eight. I'll just work on my paperwork Sunday while the store is closed." *Usually, I can't hold a normal conversation with this man. Today I'm casually discussing sex with him. This is so weird.*

"Or, we can just do it now," Luciano winked at her.

Kaylee almost jumped to her feet and agreed, but then she glanced at the clock and realized she had to get ready for work soon.

"I have to work, I can't."

"I was kidding but the fact that you almost agreed has me burning up. I need to head out before I change your mind."

Luciano rose to his feet, Kaylee followed his lead standing as well and noticed a little bounce in her step. She watched in anticipation as he leaned down to touch his soft lips to hers, coaxing them open for a kiss. The moment she opened up for him, Luciano took the kiss to the next level, deepening it, owning her mouth. His arms hugged her tightly against his body and she felt the long, hard erection growing in his pants.

He felt hot and tasted hotter.

Then just like that, he pulled away and said, "Go get dressed. I'll meet you in the car so I can take you to pick your car up at the restaurant."

Then he turned and walked out the door.

Chapter Five

What the hell is wrong with me? Kaylee had just told him what every man wants to hear. She wanted to have sex with him, no-strings-attached. So why did he feel so pissed off?

Kaylee shocked the hell out of him when she told him he was part of some plan for her to bring a little excitement into her life. That sounded damn good. The part that pissed him off was the whole in-my-spare-time thing. Granted, he didn't have a lot of time for other people, but rarely did someone not have time for him.

It didn't feel good. So he'd made the split second decision to have dinner with her. Chalking it up to not wanting to take advantage of her, he started his car and continued to wait. Kaylee may think she only wanted a sexual relationship with him, but if there was one thing he knew, it was women. Women wanted to be wined and dined. Kaylee included.

What he didn't know was why he felt so compelled to claim her before he left the apartment. He wanted her to know exactly the kind of pleasure in store for her. He needed her to remember how bad she wanted him. *I sound like a fucking Neanderthal.* A Neanderthal in pretty bad shape. Before she made it to the car, he needed to find a way to calm down. Any more excitement and he would bust his zipper.

"Fuck," Luciano said resituating himself in the seat. He wanted her, and she wanted him. He would have her Monday night, so what the hell was the problem? Why was he sulking in his car like a child who had been told he couldn't have his favorite toy for five minutes?

No doubt, Kaylee would be his favorite toy. Soon he would finally have her. He just had to keep reminding himself of the fact that it was temporary.

"So, what called on the emergency get-together tonight?" Tabby asked after she let herself into Kaylee's apartment that evening. Bri already sat on the couch making herself comfortable.

"I kissed Luciano!" Kaylee blurted out. She hadn't planned on telling them quite so bluntly but she couldn't hold it back any longer.

Brianna immediately sat up on the couch and cheered, "Holy shit. Good for you Kay."

Tab still stood in the doorway with her mouth hanging open. Kaylee could understand her friend's astonishment. She wasn't the type to kiss a man and then blab to her friends about it.

Tabby's gaze softened into a happily-ever-after smile and rushed over to Kaylee hugging her. After her hug she plopped down on the floor in front of Kaylee saying, "Tell us all about it."

"Settle down, girl. It's not like she proposed to the guy or anything," Bri told her.

"You were just as excited as me!" Tabby defended herself.

"Both of you settle down so I can tell the dang story. I'm getting antsy." Folding her legs under herself Kaylee made herself comfortable before beginning her story.

"I was outside waiting for my cab to come after the two of you left when Luciano and Nico came out. Nico left and Luciano came up to talk with me. Before I knew it he was driving me home.

"I'm telling you, I had a hard time holding it together while sitting in the car with him. You know I always turn into a crazy person when he's around. Add a little alcohol into it, and I was seriously scared."

"How'd it go?" Tabby asked.

"Not too bad actually. Besides the fact that I made him pass my own house that is." Kaylee couldn't help but laugh. Last night, it hadn't been amusing at all. Today, it was funny.

"You didn't?" Bri asked.

"I did. But you haven't heard the worst part yet," Kaylee continued. "Anyway, after we made it home. Luciano walked me to the door. I just knew this was my one and only opportunity. So, I leaned in and kissed him." It sounded so much easier while she re-told the story than it had when it actually happened. At the time, it hadn't been easy at all.

"What'd he do?" Both Tab and Bri asked in unison.

"At first he kissed me back."

"What do you mean at first?" Bri asked.

"Well, after a few seconds, he pulled away."

"He what?" Both women spoke together again.

"Are you guys sharing one brain today or what?" Kaylee unfolded her legs. "Let me finish. Yes he pulled away and my initial reaction was the same as yours. I freaked.

"Seriously. I started going off about wanting him so bad then finally getting the courage to go for him, and then how it felt to get turned down. To top it all off, after I let loose on him, I turned to walk away and ran into my front door."

Both Tabby and Bri sat staring at Kaylee for a good five seconds. Then they both burst out laughing.

Kaylee had to hold back herself. She didn't want to egg her friends on any more, but the whole story was pretty damned funny.

After the giggling ended, Tabby turned serious. "I'm sorry it turned out so bad, sweetie."

"Just wait, there's more." The excitement started to get the best of Kaylee. "First thing in the morning, guess who was back at my door?"

"No?" Tab rose to sit on her knees.

"Yes. He came back to tell me he only pulled away because I was so shitfaced. Then he told me he wanted me! I was floored." Kaylee skipped the part about throwing up and calling him the Italian Stud. She didn't want to give them any more reason to tease her.

"I'm not surprised," Bri said. "I told you that man wanted to break himself off a piece of chocolate."

"I'm ignoring you, Brianna," Kaylee said before finishing her story. "Then he started to go into that whole guy thing about not taking sex to mean more than it is. You would have been so proud of me Bri. I totally took over. I told him that I didn't want a relationship, that *I* was just out for a bit of fun and that I wanted to do it with him."

Kaylee felt proud of herself. "So to make a long story, well…shorter, he's picking me up for dinner Monday night."

"You're a girl after my own heart, Kay. I love that you two talked and decided you'd go to dinner and then have each other for dessert." Bri said bluntly.

"I'm pretty proud of myself too."

"I'm worried about you, Kay. Do you really think you can keep your feelings out of this?" Tabby asked.

"Of course I can. You know how I feel about getting my feelings involved with a man. I just can't risk it. I'm not my mother. I refuse to ever be dependent on a man for my happiness." Mom did enough of that for the both of them. Kaylee learned at a young age that "love" never lasted.

"Famous last words," Tab replied.

The whole day Kaylee's body buzzed with excitement. Tonight her fantasies would come true. Whenever she felt any nervousness trying to squeeze in she reminded herself of Luciano and what he would do to her. That was enough to keep any of her fears away. This is what she wanted and now it was finally going to happen.

Between her customers, she'd spent the day organizing books and cleaning the already spotless store. She'd moved all the rollable racks of used romance books to the front because they seemed to sell the best, repriced the mystery section, and prepared the new releases that would come out tomorrow.

Now, it was 7:30. After getting out of the shower she slipped on her red bra and panties. Wearing sexy lingerie under her clothes always made her feel hot, more womanly, like she knew a secret no one else knew. Tonight, Luciano would know that secret, too.

Her dress was a deep burgundy color; she loved the red against her dark skin. It reached her knees, had three quarter length sleeves, and a plunging neck line. A girl has to show off what she's got, and her cleavage was one thing she knew she had.

Heading back to the bathroom, Kaylee put on a light brush of make-up. A brownish-red graced her eyelids, mascara, and eye liner finished off the look. She never wore more than that, and hardly ever went that far. Taking one last glance in the mirror, she knew she looked hot.

At 7:45, Kaylee sat on her couch to wait for the Italian stud. He knocked at exactly 8:00 PM. A smile crept across her nervous face when she noticed the time. He was prompt, just like her. That idea eased the knots that formed in her stomach while she sat waiting for him. Standing up, she straightened her dress, said a quick prayer, and opened the door to the most beautiful man she had ever seen.

The epitome of gorgeous, Luciano leaned against the railing outside, staring at her. His jet-black hair hung loose reaching his collar. His strong, masculine frame filled out a charcoal gray dress shirt and a pair of black slacks. He looked hot. Heat radiated from his body so strongly it singed her already heightened senses.

Her eyes locked with his, their dark brown depths claiming her, making her unable to turn away, she didn't want to turn away. His eyes held her in a trance. Not knowing what to say, she stood there staring, hoping he would speak first.

Time almost stopped. Luciano didn't speak but stepped towards her in slow motion, grabbing her hand, and pulling her against him. He lowered his lips and kissed the tip of her nose with his firm, sensual lips.

"Does it hurt?" he finally asked. His rich, smooth, baritone danced on the notes of music.

"Hurt?" she asked dreamily.

"Your nose. Does it still hurt?"

With Luciano holding her so close, she could hardly think. Hurt? Nothing hurt right now. In his arms, she was in her own utopia, where nothing hurt, and nothing could go wrong.

"Bella?" he asked. "Does it hurt?"

Kaylee mustered the sense to respond. "No, its fine."

"You look good enough to eat." Luciano leaned close to her ear when he spoke.

"That sounds nice." The words snuck out of her mouth, she couldn't have stopped them.

"I almost want to skip dinner and feast from your lips instead."

"Really?" Kaylee asked lowering her hands.

Luciano didn't answer with words but bent and captured her mouth with his. His tongue slipped past her parted lips right where she wanted him. Damn he knew how to kiss. Slow and seductively, his tongued danced with hers.

Kaylee sighed deep into his mouth as his hands started to rub her back, moving lower and lower until he cupped her behind. He didn't stop there. Luciano gave her a squeeze causing Kaylee to feel dizzy with lust.

Damn he's good. No man had ever talked to her like he did; much less kiss her like he did. It wasn't like she was a virgin, but Luciano made her feel so much different than any other man had. Just his lips and hands took her to whole new heights of pleasure. She felt savored as he explored her body and mouth. No one had savored her before.

When the kiss ended, Kaylee wanted to faint. Right here, right now, she could pass out at any moment.

"Yes Bella. I'm on fire here. When you say things like that to me I come damn close to exploding. Add that sexy little sigh like you do, and I'm a goner." He smiled. "But I did promise you a nice dinner and I intend to keep my promise."

Kaylee and Luciano arrived at an up-scale seafood restaurant a short while later. After Luciano parked his black Mercedes, he left his seat and walked around to open Kaylee's door for her. Her hand sizzled as he grabbed it with his own to help her out of the car. Before she could walk towards the restaurant, he stopped her, pinning her against his car with that long, lean body of his.

"Did I tell you how great you look tonight?" he asked.

Kaylee flushed. She couldn't help it. She always seemed to do it in his presence. "Yes," she finally replied.

"Well I'm telling you again," he said as he started running his hands up and down her arms leaving goose bumps in his wake.

Kaylee felt the hard length of his erection as he moved against her body. He was a big man, and he was turned on...by her. The knowledge gave her the courage to rise up on her tip toes and brush her lips against his. Luciano took full advantage, kissing her back, working his magic with an urgency she hadn't felt from him before.

Kaylee wrapped her arms around his neck trying to get as close to him as possible. He tasted like the sweetest sin. As she started running her fingers through his hair, something she had always wanted to do. Luciano growled as he thrust his tongue in her mouth once more before pulling away.

"We can't do this out here, Bella. Give me a minute to cool off before we go inside."

Kaylee's disappointment must have shown on her face because he than said, "We will finish it." His voice was tense yet firm.

She didn't doubt a single word he said, but she wanted to finish it now. She wanted more. Just being so close to Luciano sent tingles of delight throughout her body. He was obviously a very passionate man. Only a couple more hours until she would know first hand just how passionate he could be.

Grabbing her hand, Luciano led her away from his parked car and into the restaurant. The eyes of half the women in the restaurant took in the sight of the handsome man on her arm as the hostess led them to their table.

Her inner pre-teen wanted to stick her tongue out at all them saying, *nana, nana, boo, boo,* but of course she didn't. Kaylee held her head high as she walked past the gawking women. For this night, Luciano was her man.

She planned to enjoy every millisecond of it. From the way he walked her to their table, to the way he pulled her chair out for her, to the way he kissed her, and would soon kiss her again. She felt beautiful, alive, sexy, and most importantly, free.

Something she never allowed herself to feel before this moment.

Luciano shifted uncomfortably in the padded restaurant chair. In all actuality, the chair probably wasn't as bad as it felt to him, but he was edgy, anxious, hard as steel. Any moment now he feared he might burst free from behind his binding zipper. Owning a restaurant himself, he knew they frowned upon that.

But damn she looked hot. Her braids were tight and silky as ever. A light amount of makeup graced her face, not too much, but just right. Her striking, wide eyes ate him up each time she looked at him. Each time she moved, the sweet smell of vanilla wrapped around him making him harder.

But her lips, oh God he couldn't get enough of them. They were ripe, red, and full. She had the most kissable mouth he had ever seen. Maybe, just maybe he could handle that, but the knock-out red dress she wore, that sent him over the edge. The perfect swells of her ample breasts peaked out, begging to be touched. She picked the right dress to mold against her soft, rounded curves.

Curves he couldn't wait to explore with his hands, his lips, his tongue. Not one inch of her body would go untouched. Not one second would go by where she wasn't writhing in pleasure beneath him, anyway he could have her. Then, maybe he'd have her out of his system.

"Can I get you anything to drink?" the blonde waitress with big hair asked, her eyes not leaving Luciano.

"Kaylee?" Luciano asked before answering the waitress.

"I'll just have water, thanks," *Better not risk spilling something that will stain.* She felt at ease, but that could change at any minute. *Around Luciano she was yo-yo bouncing back and forth between normal and loony. Who knew sexual frustration could have such damaging affects?*

"Just waters for both of us," Luciano told the flaunt fox who couldn't help but push her breasts out when he looked at her.

Kaylee wanted to yank one of her extensions out, hard. Whoever put the damn things in didn't know what they were doing.

"Are you sure?" she asked. "I could bring you out some—"

"Yes! He's sure," Kaylee said pissed at the waitress but even more mad at herself for letting her annoyance show.

"I'll be back in a moment," Blondie said as she walked away from the table.

Or, not, Kaylee thought but didn't say a word. Not with the look Luciano sent her way. His eyes penetrated her making her feel like covering herself, like he could see something she didn't want him to see.

"Sorry. People like that drive me crazy. I know this is just about sex, but *she* doesn't know that." *This kind of sucked.* Why did she say anything? "I had no right to get testy with her. It won't happen again." *As long as that waitress doesn't come back that is.*

"Don't be sorry. I would have done the same thing in your place."

"Good, now that my little outburst is out of the way, I'm going to check out the menu." Kaylee sat behind the menu wishing this meal would hurry up and get over. She'd waited six months to have Luciano, now waiting through dinner felt like too long.

A few minutes later their new waitress came out to take their orders. Apparently Blondie had to take a break. Kaylee ordered shrimp scampi while Luciano picked out lobster.

"So, were you raised in San Francisco?" Luciano asked over their meal.

"If you can call it that."

"What does that mean?"

"Nothing. I don't know why I said it. Yes, I've lived here my whole life. How about you?" *Wow that snuck out*, Kaylee thought. She didn't usually give people any insight into her past. Tabby and Bri were the only people who knew she felt more like she raised her mom than the other way around.

"My parents moved here from Italy right before I was born."

"How old are you?" Huh, it was kind of fun getting some insight to the Italian Stud.

"I'm thirty."

"You and Nico seem to be good friends. Have you been friends long?"

"We're cousins. Nico's parents were already in San Francisco so I guess mine followed along."

"Have you always been close?" If she kept asking him questions, maybe he wouldn't get around to asking her as many.

"Yeah, we're more like brothers. Nic's twenty-nine. I'm an only child, and Nic's the only son in his family. So it helped to have each other around."

The conversation was easy and the more they talked, the more relaxed she felt. Luciano seemed willing to talk and she was willing to listen. His life really fascinated her. She didn't know what it felt like to have family like he did. Even though he didn't have brothers and sisters, he had his parents, aunts, uncles, and cousins.

She felt envious of that. Until she met Tabby and Bri, she only had her mom, and that didn't count for much. She spent too much time worrying about whatever current boyfriend she had to have time to worry about Kaylee. She'd missed out on a lot of things but she couldn't change it now. What's the point in thinking about it?

"How many sisters does Nico have?" she asked.

"He's the oldest with three little sisters running around. Well, they aren't so little any more, but you'd think so the way he acts. You'd think he wouldn't be such a compulsive dater having three sisters. He'd freak if they ever brought home a guy like himself."

"Typical male," Kaylee teased. "Its okay for you to enjoy sex and dating, but not for a woman."

"Believe me, Kaylee, I want you to enjoy sex."

Heat rushed over her body so strong, she knew it oozed from her pores. Oh yeah, she'd enjoy sex with him alright and couldn't wait to have it. Hopefully they'd finish this food soon and could be on their way.

"Is everything okay?"

Great. Blondie's off her break. Kaylee thought.

"Kaylee, are you okay? Do you need anything?" Luciano asked her.

"Everything's great, thanks."

After the waitress left the table, Kaylee continued her barrage of questions. Since they were at the restaurant still and couldn't get down to business, there was no use continuing where the previous conversation headed. No point getting hot and bothered until Luciano could put out the fire.

"How long have you owned *Luciano's*?"

Kaylee watched a mixture of emotions cross his face. Initially, an extreme sadness creased his brow, making his eyes shine brightly. Somehow, she could read this man. Maybe because she had seen the same look in the mirror, sadness you hide inside to ease the pain.

As quickly as the emotions appeared on his face, they disappeared, replaced by pride. Pride in what she assumed was his restaurant because she felt the same way about *Bookends*.

"The restaurant has been mine since I was twenty-two. I started grad school at the time so we actually had to let it close for a couple years. That hurt, but once I finished business school, I opened her up again. That's been about six years now, she's been my life ever since."

"Why is it men always make their possessions women?" Kaylee asked with a laugh.

Luciano laughed as well. His strong, sexy voice vibrated the butterflies that resided in her stomach.

"I guess it's because the restaurant is pretty much my life. If I call it a her, at least I feel like there's a woman in my life."

"Well, I guess that makes Bookends a male then," Kaylee smiled her wide smile.

Kaylee really wanted to ask how Luciano ended up with the restaurant before he should have, but wasn't sure if she should. Curiosity won out, he seemed so open with her anyway, what could it hurt?

"Was Luciano's passed down to you?"

"That, Bella," Luciano said. "Is a story for another time. I think it's your turn now. Tell me about *Bookends*."

He asked the one question she didn't mind talking about. Somehow, she wondered if he knew that, but dismissed the fleeting thought. How could he know? She hadn't been too forthcoming with the details on her life.

"I've always wanted to own my own business. You know, the whole control thing," she kidded. "I saved up all the money I could afford while in college and then while I worked dead end jobs. As soon as I was able, I put a down payment down. It worked out perfect that I found a place with an apartment above. That way I kill two birds with one stone."

"What's with the whole control thing?"

She wondered if they should even be playing this whole, getting-to-know-each-other game. Wouldn't that just form the strings that neither of them wanted? This was about sex. He was a way to sate her desire as she was to him.

"Why are we doing this, Luciano? I thought we decided-"

Luciano reached across the table, putting a long, masculine finger against her lips.

"Shh. The same rules still apply. We're just making it seem a little less like what it really is."

So far, he had hushed her twice with his finger. This time, she didn't plan to let him get away with it. Quickly, and seductively, Kaylee pushed out her pink tongue and swirled it around his finger before drawing it into her mouth. She only held it there a few seconds, not wanting to make a scene. The second she released his finger, Luciano grabbed the attention of the first waiter that walked by.

"Check please."

As Kaylee stood up her hand bumped into the bottle of cocktail sauce sitting on their table knocking it over. Luckily the semi-thick liquid didn't get a chance to spill out before she grabbed it, setting the bottle upright.

Only one near spill tonight. *That isn't too bad if I do say so myself.* Now if she could get to the sex part without any mishaps.

Chapter Six

Kaylee watched Luciano sitting tensely in his seat while driving back to her apartment. He had yet to say a word since they'd gotten in the car. The fifteen minute drive seemed an eternity. The longer they drove, the more nervous Kaylee became.

I can do this. I will do this. I know I'll enjoy it, and I deserve to enjoy myself.

The closer they got to her place, the more the butterflies in her stomach were slam dancing. The apex of her thighs already tingled in anticipation.

A minute later Luciano pulled up against the curb in front of *Bookends*. Shaky fingers fumbled with the seatbelt from nerves.

"Shit," Kaylee said in a shaky voice as her fingers slipped off the belt catching her nail and bending it back.

Luciano reached down and unhooked the belt, then grabbed her hand before kissing her injured finger.

"Don't be nervous, Bella. Do you realize that the whole time we ate dinner, you didn't spill one drink? You didn't trip once. The only near accident was the cocktail sauce and I don't count that. There's no reason to be nervous anymore."

When he said that, she felt like more of a ditz, but appreciated his attempt. He was right. At dinner she'd felt like she would have if talking with anyone else. Only a couple of times through the whole dinner did her nerves stand on end but nothing compared to what they usually did around him.

Taking a couple of deep breaths Kaylee looked into Luciano's eyes as he held tightly to her hand. He looked so sincere, and so damn hot. She let her eyes wander down his chest and they fell to his lap. He already sported a hard-on while she sat here quaking in her heels.

Her eyes held on the impressive bulge in his pants when she saw him pulse, quickly jutting out the materiel of his pants.

She licked her lips.

His bulge grew.

Her nerves eased.

"Race you to the door," Kaylee said before opening the car, and making a mad dash for the stairs on the side of the building. Her impatience to have him surged with each step.

Luciano managed to catch up to her halfway up the stairs.

"Ahh. What are you doing?" Kaylee screamed as Luciano lifted her into his arms and ran up the rest of the stairs. No one had ever picked her up like this. As she bounced in his arms while he ran up the stairs, she couldn't help but laugh.

"Speeding up the process," Luciano told her. "I don't want to risk any accidents."

"Hey. That's not funny." Kaylee playfully smacked him in the arm before opening her purse to get her keys. "I guess you better do this part too, Mr. Comedian. We wouldn't want to risk me running into the door again."

"No." He took the keys. "I was just kidding. It's smooth sailing from here on out."

"I know. Don't worry, I don't get my feelings hurt that easy." When he smiled she continued, "Hurry up and open the door. I don't know if I've ever told you, but I'm extremely impatient."

"I'm going, I'm going." Luciano unlocked her house with Kaylee still in his arms. Once inside her dark apartment, he set her on her feet and turned to lock the door.

"Lead the way," he told her.

The second they reached her room, Luciano attacked her in a pleasure filled assault. His mouth covered hers, his tongue demanding entrance. Luciano's usually steady hands began to fumble with the zipper on the back of her dress. The damn thing wouldn't budge but her courage soared at his enthusiasm.

As if he couldn't get enough of her, Luciano raised one trembling hand to the back of her head holding her close while his tongue danced in her mouth. The kiss wasn't like any they'd shared before. It went beyond urgent into the unfamiliar territory of need. Kaylee pulled away with a jerk when the word popped into her mind.

"What's wrong? Am I going too fast?" Luciano shook his head. "I want you so bad right now."

His words reignited the fire burning inside her. She wanted him too, more than words could explain. This was only about sex, and they both knew it so there wasn't any reason to freak out.

"I want you too, Luciano," Kaylee said before standing on her tiptoes to kiss him once more. She felt Luciano's hesitancy, his kiss still sweet, but softer than before.

"It's okay," she whispered against his lips. "Don't hold back."

He needed no more convincing. His tongue mated with hers. How did this man always taste like sweet Italian herbs? Kaylee wrapped her arms around his neck wanting to feel the heat of his body against every inch of hers. His body molded perfectly along hers as he started to grind his hips, rubbing his long, hard erection on her belly, his lips now trailing sensual kisses across her jaw and down her neck.

"Luciano," she whispered past her lips. Kaylee felt on the verge of an explosion. She burned for him. The butterflies were gone, replaced by a heavy ache for Luciano. Kaylee felt her head flop back in a request for him to keep going.

The zipper was stuck. Luciano worked away at it while kissing and nipping at her neck.

"Is this one of your favorite dresses?" Luciano asked.

"No. I usually don't do dresses. Only lately." His breath was tickling her skin.

"Good," Luciano replied. "You look hot in this sexy dress, but its holding me back."

Luciano's strong hands grasped the fabric and pulled causing the dress to rip at the zipper. First shock and then laughter bubbled inside her until it overflowed and she couldn't control the sound. Her shoulders shook up and down while Luciano continued to kiss her, finally lowering the dress from her shoulders and capturing her peaked nipple through her bra.

That quieted the laughter.

Kaylee let a sigh move past her lips and into the air. She heard Luciano growl as he nipped at her pebbled bud then grabbed the cup of her bra with his teeth and pulled it under her breast.

Wet warmth enveloped Kaylee's breast. Then he lowered the other cup. Luciano went back and forth between each breast, Kaylee holding the back of his head firmly in place. She let her hands run through his silky hair as her pleasure built inside of her.

Luciano's hand traveled down her side, and over her hip, before sneaking under the dress at her waist, Kaylee felt her whole body shiver in anticipation. When he cupped her butt she had to hold back from letting go right there.

Not yet, she told herself. Slowly his hand dipped under her panties and down her center before he pushed one finger inside her. He began pumping it in and out. Her internal muscles clutched around him.

"You feel so good," Luciano told her.

Words escaped her. The sensations were too strong to form any kind of coherent sentence. Kaylee moaned letting him know she agreed.

He licked and sucked on her breasts, while his finger treated her to even more pleasure. Kaylee couldn't hold back any longer. Pleasure flooded her body as her legs tightened around his hand. Letting loose, she screamed in climax.

"God, you're hot," Luciano said as he inched Kaylee backwards towards her bed. When her knees bumped the side, she fell, her arms still wrapped around him, he toppled with her.

Her contagious laughter ignited his own. Damn she was fun. He couldn't remember a time when he'd laughed as much as he did around her. She felt like a high, one he'd never experienced.

Looking down, Luciano spotted her perked dark brown nipples begging for his mouth once again. He couldn't resist and lowered his face to her offering. She tasted hot and sweet like fudge. He knew at that moment he'd need seconds, maybe thirds before he had his fill of her.

He planned to take his time with her but his cock had other ideas. He wanted to join in the fun something fierce. Luciano had waited too long to deny himself. The anticipation almost killed him.

"I can't wait anymore, Bella. I have to have you now." Luciano stood grabbing the ripped dress balled at her waist and pulled it off. A flash of hesitation appeared in her honey brown eyes. Luciano smiled, and the hesitation was gone, replaced by lust.

Never had he wanted a woman this much. As her dark body lay against the white blanket he knew he was looking at the most beautiful woman he would ever see. Her sexy, voluptuous body called out to him on a level he didn't understand.

"Lean forward," he commanded.

Kaylee did. Luciano reached behind her unhooking the sexy red bra freeing her breasts. They were more than a handful and he couldn't wait to touch them again. First, he had other business to attend to.

Kneeling in front of her, Luciano hooked his fingers in her matching panties and slowly pulled them down her legs. Her musky feminine scent mixed with the smell of vanilla. Luciano leaned towards her body inhaling her, locking her scent into his senses. His body ached for release within her.

"I want to explore every inch of you, Kaylee, find all your hidden treasures. But if I don't get inside you right now, I'm going to embarrass myself."

He reached into his pants pocket and pulled out a condom.

Kaylee's tongue had a mind of its own as she watched Luciano remove his shirt. She licked her lips in anticipation for the show he unknowingly put on for her. As he pulled the shirt open she got her first glimpse of the man beneath.

His smooth olive skin, stretched tight against firm muscles. A light dusting of black hair covered his chest and six-pack abs. She had to physically hold herself back from touching.

As the shirt hit the floor, she saw the firm arms that carried her up the stairs earlier. They were long, and strong.

Then his hands moved to the button on his pants. The rest of the world ceased to exist as he unbuttoned his pants and lowered the zipper. As if he sensed her desire and curiosity, Luciano pushed his pants down his legs and pulled on the condom in one quick, fluid movement.

His arms weren't the only thing long and strong on his body.

God I picked the perfect man to put some excitement in my life, Kaylee thought as she crawled backwards to the head of the bed ready for the Italian Stud.

Crack!

"Ouch," Kaylee squealed as she bonked the back of her head on the headboard. "I need to take out an accident policy when you're around. This is getting dangerous."

Luciano smiled. "My God you're a breath of fresh air, you know that?" he asked as he climbed naked on the bed towards her.

"Why? Because I give a good laugh?" Kaylee continued to rub her head.

"You're fun," was all he said as he bent forward and pressed a sweet kiss to her head. "Feel better?"

At that moment, Kaylee forgot all about her throbbing head. A sexy, naked, hard man leaned over her, a man she'd wanted for six months.

"Does what feel better?" Kaylee asked as she grabbed his butt and pull him between her legs.

"Nothing," Luciano said, his voice husky before he lowered his lips to hers, and eased his way into her body at the same time.

Luciano growled in what she hoped was approval.

Kaylee sighed.

He began to pump inside her, filling her up. Bursts of pleasure shot though her body filling her with bliss from his rock-hard length inside of her. He electrified her, delighted her body in ways she'd never experienced, ways she could get used to experiencing.

He rocked his body in and out, his lips still kissing her sweetly. As pleasure began to increase she rode the wave higher and higher into ecstasy until she hit a peak and let loose a powerful release strong enough to bring down the walls.

As she shuttered, riding out the aftershocks of her climax, Luciano tensed, his body pulsed, and he let loose a moan along with a climax of his own.

Kaylee awoke with a start, sweat beading on her forehead, and Luciano's arms wrapped around her, holding her. He felt warm and comfortable and that scared her to death.

Thank God her dream awakened her. Kaylee lay there as memories of her childhood played in her head. They were as vivid as if they had happened just yesterday. She remembered being disgusted. How could her mom not see what her twelve year old daughter could see?

God how she'd begged her mom not to let her new "love" move in with them. Even at that young age she'd been independent, offering to help her mom anyway she could just so it could be the two of them. But Mom said there were more ways than one a woman needed to be taken care of.

I'm not like my mom. I don't need a man to hold me at night.

Kaylee moved out from under his warmth, shaking Luciano awake.

"Luciano, we fell asleep. You have to go." She could hear the pleading in her own voice.

"Come here," he replied. "We can go back to sleep for awhile before we start again. I'm not done with you yet," his voice held a promise that her body wanted to give into, but she couldn't.

"We're done for tonight. I need you to get up," she said poking him. "You can't sleep here." She didn't need a man to hold her at night. She wasn't her mother.

Finally Luciano opened his eyes, really hearing what she said.

"Is something wrong?" he asked.

Pain washed over her at the wary look in his eyes. If only she could let him stay, if only she could let him hold her, kiss her, and make love to her over and over. She didn't dare.

"No you didn't do anything wrong, I just need you to go. What we have is about sex, not about holding each other, and spending the night."

"I didn't ask you to marry me, Kaylee. I just wanted to lay here with you."

"Listen," Kaylee crossed her arms over her chest. "No changing the rules now. You wanted it like this just as much as I did."

Luciano sat up, naked and gorgeous.

"I'm not changing any rules, Bella. This is still about sex, but I didn't know I'd get kicked out afterwards."

"I'm sorry. I should have explained to you. I don't do the whole, spend the night, holding each other and talking about our feelings thing. If you plan to continue this, you have to know that I don't work that way." Even to her own ears it sounded harsh. "I have to work in the morning so I don't need to be up all night either. My job is the most important thing to me, Luciano. I know you understand that."

She saw a light click in his dark eyes. "You're right, Kaylee. I do understand that. I'll be out of here in a few minutes."

Luciano left her bed, picked up his clothes and headed to the bathroom.

She missed his presence already.

Luciano lay in his bed thinking about Kaylee. They had so much fun together. She was smart, funny, and sexy as hell. He enjoyed spending time with her more than he wanted to admit, even to himself.

Something unusual came over him tonight, some unfamiliar longing to hold her, and caress her all night long. He hadn't wanted to do that with a woman, ever, but for some reason, he'd come close tonight. Thank God Kaylee brought him to his senses.

When she first woke him practically pushing him from her bed he was pissed. He'd barely begun and she was kicking him out. Then like a smack in the face, he realized she was right. They were having sex, not a relationship. There wasn't going to be any cuddling afterwards and talking of feelings. That created strings and strings were bad.

So why couldn't he sleep? Why was he sitting in bed wishing she was there with him? The only answer that he could come up with was that his body needed more than just once with her. He would need to have her a few more times, take his time with her. Maybe after a few more nights together, he'd be through. That's all either of their lives would let them have anyway.

He realized tonight that he'd been dead wrong about Kaylee. They were more alike than he wanted to think about. Her walls were built just as high as his own, her life just as business oriented, just as shut off from emotions. It hurt to think about it—a woman like her living the kind of life he did. Sure all work and no play fitted him. But despite what Kaylee thought, it didn't fit her. She deserved more. Too bad he'd never be able to give it to her.

Chapter Seven

After a night spent surfing the internet for the meaning of the word, Bella, Kaylee finally accepted the fact that she wouldn't be getting any sleep tonight. She'd spent the last few hours tossing and turning in bed. She felt guilty about the way she'd thrown Luciano out but knew it to be for the best. Still, when a man gave you two orgasms in one night and called you beautiful in his native tongue, it had to be bad etiquette to send him packing, right?

That's exactly what she'd done. Kicked him out then suffered for it the rest of the night. Kaylee walked to her bedroom with coffee in hand, looking for something comfy to wear to work today. With any luck she'd be able to hold her eyes open the whole day. If she kept herself busy it shouldn't be a problem. She still had lists of things to get accomplished at *Bookends*, so the added incentive to work her thoughts away was welcomed.

She needed any and everything she could think about to help her forget the way Luciano made her feel. Thinking about it, she might do something crazy like call him over to do it again. This time, she wouldn't fall asleep afterwards. She'd never allowed herself to spend the whole night with a man. She had sex, but never actually slept with anyone. That was until the night before when she'd fallen asleep for an hour or so within Luciano's embrace.

Sleeping with someone formed a connection she never wanted. Unlike her mom, she didn't need a man to take care of her or to hold her through the night. She and Luciano shared a desire for one another and a means to add something exciting to their busy, work-oriented lives. That's all.

Kaylee sat on the edge of her messy bed sipping her coffee, remembering what Luciano had done to her. As if burned by the warm blanket beneath her she leapt from the bed, spilling a bit of hot coffee on her sheets.

Great, just great, she thought. *Now I'm becoming clumsy just from thinking about him.* Maybe the sex made things worse? No way. She refused to let that thought creep into her head. What she did last night couldn't make anything worse. It felt too good.

Kaylee moved to her chest of drawers, setting her coffee down and grabbing a pair of blue jeans, a purple v-neck shirt, and her purple lingerie before heading to the bathroom for a quick shower. She hoped to wash the memories away and then head down to the store for a nice long day of work.

"How'd it go last night, girl?" Bri asked after she and Tabby walked into *Bookends* mid-morning.

"How'd what go?" Kaylee played coy but she didn't fool anyone, least of all herself. Last night had been a blast, the dinner, the talking, the sex. Everything had been wonderful until she went and had a meltdown.

"You know exactly what we're talking about," Tab added. "Now spill."

"Girl talk in the middle of my bookstore? Great idea," Kaylee kidded.

"Quit stalling. I'll use force if necessary," Bri added.

"How do you think it went? He was great," Kaylee finally told them. Maybe a little too great. "We had dinner at a seafood place. The food was great. Luciano talked about his restaurant, a little bit about how he grew up," turning to Tabby she said, "and of course about Nico."

"Why do you look at me when you say that?" Tabby wanted to know.

"Hmm. I wonder why?" Bri laughed.

"Stop changing the subject. This is about you, Kay." Tabby obviously didn't want to admit her attraction to Nico.

"Well, I was close to my normal self," Kaylee walked down the mystery aisle and sat down on one of the couches where people sometimes sat to read. The other girls followed suit. "I didn't have my typical Luciano induced accident. There was only one minor incident the whole night. All in all we had a great time." She really didn't want to go into details with the girls. Kaylee wasn't one to kiss and tell, but they knew what happened anyway.

"That's all you're going to tell us? He must not have been that good. I'm sorry, sweetie," Bri said patting her hand.

"With a body like his, how can you doubt he'd be good, girl? I knew before he took his clothes off he'd be good. Luciano didn't disappoint." At the smile on Bri's face, Kaylee knew she'd just been had.

"You did that on purpose, didn't you?" she asked knowing the answer.

"I knew that's the only way we'd get any details, not that you gave up much." Bri laughed. "So when are you guys hooking' up again?"

"I don't know. I guess whenever time permits. We both have busy schedules. It is just sex you know."

"You're starting to sound more and more like, Bri, Kaylee," Tabby added.

"I'm just enjoying myself for once. When I'm not too busy that is."

All three girls laughed but quickly quieted when the bell over the door jingled. Kaylee jumped to her feet to help her customer. Play time was over. She had work to do.

Bookends had a busy day, something Kaylee really needed. After Brianna and Tabby left, customer after customer made their way in, the majority making purchases, which put a smile on her face. Luckily, the business made it hard to spend too much time thinking about Luciano and the way he made her feel. Her body ached in places that had been unattended for far too long. Places he'd attended to last night.

The ache not only came from the night before, but also from desire. Now that her body had found the release it sought, the craving became much more consuming. Chocolate had nothing on Luciano. His sweet body was much more addicting.

the

Three days had passed since his dinner and way too short interlude with Kaylee. Usually, women were ringing his phone off the hook by now. *When can we see each other again? I miss you.* Yada, yada, yada. Any other time, the calls and attention annoyed him, pushed him away. Now, the lack of attention was really starting to piss him off.

Luciano didn't want a relationship, but he didn't want to be ignored either. This was a first for him. He was in unfamiliar territory when it came to worrying about a woman's lack of attention. He wanted to talk to Kaylee but pride kept him from calling. Even though in the end he agreed with Kaylee's reasoning, she'd been the one to boot him out, so she should be the one to pick up the phone and give him a call. They had agreed on a sexual affair. That involved phone calls, meeting, and finding the nearest bed.

The lack of attention stung his ego a bit. First, she'd been just as willing as him to push the whole no commitment sex thing. Now, she left him hanging on when, where, and *if* he'd get to have her again. *Didn't I want distance?*

Of course he did, he just hated that she wanted it just as much, maybe even more. In a foul mood, Luciano tried to smile at the few customers in his restaurant. During the day the place didn't have the string of patrons it did during the evening.

Luciano walked from table to table, straightening the red table cloths on the empty tables and making small talk with the customers. His thoughts however remained on Kaylee. Realizing he wasn't being the best welcome party to his customers, Luciano grumbled while walking back towards his office.

The room was small with a dark wood desk, a leather reclining computer chair, and a bookshelf filled with restaurant guides and policy books. Sitting down in his chair, Luciano ran a hand through his hair in frustration. Why the hell hadn't she called? Was she turning back into the shy woman who could hardly talk to him? Did she sit in her bookstore waiting for him to call?

A knock sounded on the door bringing a bigger frown to his face. He was horny and his ego bruised, not the best combo and definitely not how he wanted to feel when he had company.

"I'm busy," Luciano said firmly to whoever stood behind his door.

The door swung open and Nico stepped inside. "Not too busy for your cousin, are you?"

Did the man ever stop smiling?

"I'm too busy for anyone right now Nic. Can it wait?"

"Sure it can, but I don't want to," Nico replied. "Feeling a little tense, are ya?"

"Since when did you become psychic? Maybe you should consider opening up a booth at the fair this year." Luciano knew he sounded irritated but didn't care.

"Testy, testy," Nico tsked.

He wasn't in the mood. "What do you need?"

"Do I need an excuse to stop by and see my favorite cousin?"

"Do I need an excuse to knock your lights out?" Luciano returned.

"What's up, Lu? You're in a lousy mood. Still not getting any? That will do it, not that I'd know." Nico laughed, but Luciano didn't.

"I'm trying to decide if I want to bite the bullet and call Kaylee." *Why did I just say that*?

"Don't call, just go over and see her."

"You don't even know the situation. How can you give advice?" Luciano looked at his cousin. Should he just go over and see Kaylee? Was he really fretting about going to see a woman?

"I may not know the situation, but I know women. Go see her. It'll do ya some good. I'll stay and watch the restaurant for a couple hours for you."

Without thinking, Luciano jumped to his feet, clapped his cousin on the back and walked out the door.

What the hell, Nico thought heading over to take a seat in Luciano's vacant chair. A smile spread across his face as he propped his feet on his cousin's desk. Luciano was finally starting to get a life. About time. When he'd made the suggestion that his cousin go see Kaylee he hadn't expected him to comply. Hell, he would have put money on just the opposite.

The restaurant meant more than anything to Luciano. Nico respected that, but he loved his cousin and wanted him to be happy. The restaurant made him happy, but not the kind of happiness Luciano deserved. After all he'd been through, he deserved real happiness. He deserved to enjoy his life.

Luciano had been an adult way too long, longer than he should have been. Nico respected him more than anyone he knew. He hated to see his fears eating him up; fears of being like his father, of hurting someone, of letting his mom down. He carried a heavy weight and Nico couldn't help but hope Kaylee could ease it.

Only one more day until Friday, one more day until she would see Luciano again. The past couple of days wrecked havoc on her hormones. Luciano put them on overdrive. Her body stood on edge all week and she knew he'd be the only cure. That knowledge kept her from calling him. The unfamiliar feeling growing within her resembled need, a need she couldn't allow herself to feel.

Luckily *Bookends* kept her busy enough that she only had time to think about him at night. The nights were hard, Mama had been right about that, but Kaylee didn't need a man to comfort her, she needed him to devour her before being on his merry way.

Which is exactly what Luciano gave her.

I'm terrible! All I care about is sex! Terrible was safe. The other alternative wasn't. *I'm a strong, independent, black woman. I don't need a man to feel my worth.* Still, she sure enjoyed the time they'd spent together. Luciano made her tingle all over, he made her feel naughty. But more importantly, he made her smile, something only Bri, Tab and her bookstore did for her.

That made him all the more dangerous. She liked him for more than the pleasure he gave her. She liked his laugh, his hard-working nature, the way he looked at her. Those emotions filled her with fear.

Walking towards the front of the store, Kaylee flipped the out to lunch sign and locked the door so she could run upstairs to get some lunch. Turning, she took two steps towards the side door when a heavy knock rattled the glass. Her stomach growled. One last customer before lunch wouldn't be too bad.

When Kaylee turned to see Luciano, her mouth raised in a smile and her breasts began to ache. He stood outside the door radiating sexy. His raven hair was tied back. He wore black jeans and a white oxford shirt with the sleeves rolled up to his elbows exposing his powerful arms. In his hand he carried a brown sack with the words *Luciano's*.

Even through the glass door that separated them she saw desire in his eyes. She knew her eyes mirrored the same feeling. Excitement surged through her body but still she stood there. Watching.

Luciano held the bag up higher and pointed. He spoke her language.

Slowly she walked to the door, unlocked it, and let him in. While she fumbled with the lock to insure their privacy she heard Luciano's deep, uneven breaths behind her.

"How long is your lunch, Bella?" he asked, his voice urgent.

"I usually just grab something to eat and then open back up. Most of the time I eat while I finish working."

"Not today," his voice commanded. "If I can take a lunch break, so can you. I'm starving," he raised his eyebrows letting her know his words had two meanings.

"Me too." *Did I really admit that*?

"Upstairs," he again ordered her.

"I don't take well to commands, Luciano. Plus, the backroom is closer." Kaylee ran past him towards the back of the store, Luciano close on her heels. She rounded the corner into her storage/office tripping over a box on the floor before falling onto the couch.

Laughter erupted from her body so strong she had to hold her stomach. Through giggles she saw Luciano standing in the doorway, watching her. His smile seductive.

"I've decided to embrace this klutz you bring out in me," she laughed. "It's actually kind of fun. When it doesn't hurt that is."

All laughter stopped as Luciano approached, kneeling over her, he rested his firm body against hers.

"How long do we have?" he asked.

"Not long," she whispered as his lips tickled her neck. His breath warming her skin. Kaylee tilted her head back allowing Luciano better access. "I…I can't think when you do that."

"How long, Bella?" he asked again. "An hour?" His breath still caressed her neck while his lips had a brief reprieve to speak.

"Thirty minutes," as she spoke, Luciano began to grind his hips against her, his erection touching her in all the right places.

"Make that forty minutes," her voice rasped.

"Fifty." Luciano moved his hand to palm her left breast.

"Forty five, not a minute longer."

"Stop thinking about your store, Kaylee." Luciano commanded before nipping her earlobe. "Just feel. Does this feel good?" he asked rolling her nipple between his long fingers.

"God, yeah."

Luciano broke their contact, grabbing her purple tank top to pull it off. Her front clasp, purple lace bra came next with a quick flick from Luciano's long fingers.

This man is good, Kaylee thought.

"Does this feel better?" he asked as the pads of his fingers creating heat and caressed her now bare breasts.

"Yes," Kaylee felt herself wiggle beneath him, trying to create as much contact as possible. Luciano felt so good tucked against her, moving his long, solid body against her own.

She could let him do this all day. Kissing her neck, shoulders, behind her ears, while his hand tended to her heavy, aching breasts. With his hands on her Kaylee forgot about the world around her. The phone rang snapping her from one of the most pleasurable moments of her life.

Luciano groaned as Kaylee pushed against his chest. "You're on your lunch break, Bella. Ignore it." He tried to kiss her, hoping she would forget the phone that he was two seconds from pulling out of the wall.

"It will only take a second."

He shut his eyes as Kaylee eased out from under him.

"Thank you for calling *Bookends*. How may I help you?"

Luciano laid there, rock hard, on edge, and for a moment, resenting her damn bookstore. He watched her talk to whoever spoke on the other end of the phone, her beautiful, dark-skinned body naked from the waist up.

She wore her braids tied up in some kind of bun on top of her head. Did she have any idea how sexy he found her? How much he hurt right now with the need to have her? Possess her? Even if it was only for, Luciano raised his arm to glance at his watch, thirty eight more minutes.

Without thinking, Luciano stood, stripped, and walked over to her slowly. He smiled. She stuttered.

"Umm. Yes, I can order that book—"

Luciano pulled her braids from the bun watching them fall against the breasts. Grabbing her hair, he pushed it over her shoulders to lie against her back. He lowered his mouth to one pert nipple and sucked.

"I...I can't look up the price right now," Kaylee said into the phone, sounding a bit breathless. "Umm. The computers," she stuttered. "They crashed. Can you..."

Luciano sucked harder, enjoying her unique taste as it tickled his tongue. "Call...back...later?"

Luciano moved to her other breast treating it to the same care. He didn't want to lose any of his time with her today. Kaylee was strong and independent. He knew she would really kick him out at the end of their forty-five minutes.

"Thanks," Kaylee hung up the phone with a loud click before grabbing his head to hold it to her chest.

"Don't think I'm letting you get away with that," she told him. "I won't tolerate—"

Luciano silenced her with his mouth. She tasted sweet. He felt like a volcano seconds to eruption.

Lowering his hand, Luciano eased into her pants and pushed one finger inside her. As soon as her muscles loosened up to accommodate him, he added another. Her body clamped tightly around his finger. Her velvety, wetness urging him on. He wanted to explode right then.

"This is much more fun than that phone call, Kaylee," he said a mere inch from her mouth. "Don't you think?"

"Yes, but Luciano—"

He didn't give her a chance to finish but again grabbed her mouth in a searing kiss. His fingers moved in and out of her warmth while she moved her hips to the same rhythm.

She panted against his mouth. "Yes. Please!"

"That's it, Bella. Enjoy yourself, let yourself go, enjoy the pleasure I'm giving you."

"I...faster, Luciano."

Luciano smiled, his erection throbbing with need, his pride soaring because of the passion he witnessed in her honey brown eyes. His body ached to possess her, to feel her tightness clamped around his cock. He needed to give her this pleasure first before he took her. Moving his fingers faster he felt her muscles begin to tighten, to pulse. His smile grew as she gripped him, her fingernails digging into his skin.

"Let loose, Kaylee."

As her name left his mouth, Kaylee came, her breathing labored before she collapsed against him.

"My time isn't quite up yet." Luciano lifted Kaylee into his arms, her legs automatically locking around his waist. He reveled in the feel of her wrapped tightly in his arms. She was warm, soft, and spent. At that moment, for the first time, he wished he didn't have to go back to work, but then, she'd still kick him out anyway.

Kaylee opened her eyes as Luciano laid her back onto the couch. Her body felt drained. Raking her eyes over Luciano, he looked primed and ready to go. His erection stood long and thick.

Luciano pulled a foil package from his pants pocket. He ripped it open with his teeth, Kaylee's eyes glued to his muscled body. When his hands moved down to sheath his length, her breath caught. Breathing? Who needed to breath at a time like this?

"Again I'm not getting the chance to take my time with you, Bella. This is going to be fast and hard," he winked. "But you'll still love it."

She didn't doubt him. Kaylee waited impatiently as Luciano stripped her. "Beautiful," he said before positioning himself between her legs, pushing inside her in one hard thrust. Kaylee's body almost burst with immediate pleasure as she called his name.

Luciano didn't move.

"Will you give me more time when we meet again, Kaylee?"

"Start moving, and I'll tell you."

"Answer me, and I'll start moving."

If he planned to wait for her to give in, it'd be a pretty long wait. "I don't know. In fact, I think we're going to have to cut it short today. I need to get back to work." *Please don't let him listen to me.*

He laughed. "No backing out now, Bella," Luciano began pumping inside her. "Don't think I'm letting this go."

"Of course not." Inside, she knew she just dodged a bullet. She couldn't give herself much more time with him at all.

"Don't forget to eat your lunch," Luciano said as he walked out the door of *Bookends* a few minutes later. "You need to re-energize yourself."

Damn that felt good.

"I won't. I'm pretty good at eating and working at the same time," she smiled. "I have to make up some of my work. I have a big book order to put in."

"Yeah, I need to get back too. I can't believe I walked out on my restaurant like I did." Luciano shook his head.

"What's the big deal? You left Nico there, didn't you?"

"How often do you leave Bri or Tabby running your store, Kaylee?" he knew that was all he had to say.

"Point taken. Now get out of here, I have some work to do," she kidded.

Luciano walked over, covering Kaylee's mouth in a scorching, rough kiss. He felt the primal urge to mark her, remind her that she was his. As the thought entered his head, he pulled abruptly away from her. *Wow. Where did that come from?* Kaylee didn't belong to anyone, least of all him. He wanted it that way, didn't he?

Pushing the ludicrous thoughts from his head he bent to lightly touch his lips to hers, softly placing a kiss on her swollen mouth. "No more rushing, Bella. Next time, I plan to savor your scrumptious little body."

Without another word to her, he turned and walked out the door.

Chapter Eight

Thirty hours had passed since Luciano came to *Bookends* for the lunch time quickie. It sounded bad calling it that, even to herself, but what else could she call it? Sometimes the truth hurt, but this happened to be a truth she wanted.

She and Luciano were having an affair. An exciting no-holds-barred, no-strings-attached, hot, sweaty, sexy affair.

You go, girl!

Surprisingly enough, the time they'd spent together, she hadn't thought about the store. Well, except for the phone call, and the whole time discussion. Other than that, he'd had her full, undivided attention. Not many people managed that but Luciano did, and hopefully he didn't even know it. *Thank God for small favors.*

Kaylee stacked a couple of boxes of used trade-in books behind the counter before double checking the lock on the front door. Hitting the light switch, she turned and walked to the side exit door. After locking up, she headed upstairs to change for Friday at *Luciano's.*

Tonight, for the first time in a long while, she wouldn't be arriving on time. Having an affair is one thing, but a girl still needs to keep her distance. Showing up thirty minutes before Bri and Tabby arrived would be dangerous. Who knows what she'd be tempted to do, despite the fact that they were in the middle of a restaurant. Hell, look what they'd done in her bookstore.

Things seemed to be working out perfectly, even better than planned. They'd met up twice, they'd had a fun time and then he went on his way. Just the way it should be. She didn't need any man to make her life worthwhile. Bookends along with Bri and Tabby were enough for her. They gave her everything she needed in life. Well, except for the killer orgasms.

Then why do I find myself wishing I had more time to spend with Luciano? It had to be the sex. She never needed or wanted a man before and Luciano wasn't any different. Right?

"What the hell?" Bri asked as she and Tabby walked up and saw Kaylee sitting outside of Luciano's. "Did I just step into the Twilight Zone?"

"Ha ha," Kaylee mocked.

"Seriously, Kay, what's up? You're always here, sitting down at the table by the time we arrive every Friday," Tabitha added.

"Nothing's up. I just had a busy day, so I couldn't get here until now. Since I knew I was as late as the two of you, I figured I'd just wait."

"Is that supposed to be a dig? If so, I'm in too good of a mood to even reply. I'm so happy it's Friday." Bri smiled and held open the door for Kay and Tab to walk in.

"I hope they didn't give our seats away, thinking we weren't coming," Tabby said scanning the dimly lit restaurant.

"Girl, there's no way those two Italian men are giving away our table," Bri told her.

As they rounded the corner into the restaurant, they discovered that in fact they hadn't given their table away. Kaylee's heart rate picked up the pace as they neared the table. For some reason her nerves had the better of her. This would be the first Friday at Luciano's since they started sleeping together.

Would Tab and Bri behave or would they find ways to embarrass her? How would Luciano act? Would Nico cause a scene? Would tonight be a rerun of all her old attack of the killer klutz episodes or could she keep her cool? Questions floated through her mind but only time would provide the answers.

"I wonder why there's a fourth seat," Bri asked.

Kaylee hadn't even noticed. Now that she did, she wondered. "Maybe they did give our seats away." *Great. Just freaking' great. What was Luciano playing at?*

"Or maybe the Italian Stud decided to join us tonight since he and Kaylee are now—" Nico walked up to the table as Bri spoke.

"Now, now, ladies, we wouldn't want to embarrass Kaylee by talking about her relationship with Luciano now would we?"

Nico stood by the table with his golden smile. His smile could probably charm the pants off of any woman in the room. Except for Kaylee, she was immune. Luciano was her drug of choice.

"Don't think that smile is going to help you get away with anything around me, Nico. I'm not embarrassed and I don't have any kind of relationship with Luciano," Kaylee said firmly.

"I beg to differ, Bella," Luciano said from behind her.

Kaylee noticed Nico's grin. Did someone turn up the heat? The restaurant suddenly felt like a smothering sauna.

Kaylee almost reached for her water to cool her down but thought better of it. No way would she risk spilling another drink. Plus, who does he think he is? Of course they didn't have a relationship.

"Really? This is a new one for me."

"Hmmm. And all this time I thought we were friends. Where I come from, friendship is a form of a relationship."

He had her there. The smile on his face told her he knew it too. The smug, sexy, jerk.

"You got me there, but I think everyone knew what I meant, Luciano," Kaylee replied in a cool, even tone.

"Not me," Nico joked.

"Me either," Bri added.

"Whoever declared this pick on Kaylee day, I'm taking' out back." Kaylee wanted to find a way to change the subject, like now.

"Is that an invitation?" Kaylee was surprised to realize it was Nico rather than Luciano who spoke. When she turned to look at him, he winked and she knew he had something up his sleeve.

Luciano replied before she had the chance. "No. It wasn't." Luciano stepped forward putting his hands on her shoulders.

"That's not what I meant and you know it, Nico." Kaylee felt uncomfortable as Luciano stood holding her shoulders, Bri and Tabby's eyes plastered to her. Why the heck was he acting all protective?

Nico started to laugh. "I'm just joking, boss, relax. You all know Tabby's the woman for me."

As if he just realized the way he behaved, Luciano stepped back, taking his warm hands from her shoulders. "I have to check on something. Make sure you give Mike a rundown of tonight's specials before you head back out."

Kaylee turned and watched Luciano walk through a door that led to the back. What the hell just happened?

❧

"Uh oh. I think Luciano's feeling a bit green," Tabby said.

Kaylee felt the goose bumps traveling across her arms. "He's not jealous, Tab. We're just friends and everyone knows it."

Luciano had acted jealous though, but that didn't make any sense. They slept together, it was only sex and they both knew it. Why would he be jealous over Nico? Even though the idea excited her in some ways, it scared her more.

"Sure thing, Babe. Think what you want," Nico winked at her.

"Why do we have a fourth chair tonight?" Tabby asked.

Kaylee noticed a slight twinkle as she looked at Nico.

"You won't give me a date, sweetheart, so I'm taking one," Nico replied to Tabby while Kaylee sat back and enjoyed the show. She enjoyed seeing someone else in the hot seat for once.

"You are, are you? This is supposed to be girl's night out." Tabby replied.

"I sit with you every Friday night," Nico countered.

"Not the whole night! Don't you have to work?"

"Nope. We hired a new part-time chef. Tonight he's running the show by himself so we can see how he does. Give me about ten minutes to go over a few things with him, and I'm all yours." Nico bent down towards her ear to speak. "And I do mean that, sweetheart."

"What is with these guys?" Kaylee asked. Both Nico and Luciano had thrown them for a loop tonight.

"They want you. Sex will do that to a man," Bri said nonchalantly.

"But I'm not having sex with Nico!" Tabby said in a slightly raised voice. "And from what I hear, he has plenty other women. So why's he bothering me?"

"Because you turn him down, girl. Men like that aren't used to being turned down. Have sex with him once and he'll be off your back," Brianna answered.

"Bri!" Tabby and Kaylee both said in unison.

"I'm kidding. You guys need to chill," Bri said and took a drink of her martini. Somehow the waitress had brought them out without them noticing. "Nico's a flirt but I don't think he's that bad. I'm sure he knows how to enjoy himself, but I don't think he's out there screwing every chick in town."

"Great way to put it, Brianna," Kaylee replied.

"He flirts with every woman that walks in here, Bri. I don't know why he doesn't leave me alone. He knows I'm not like that." Tabby downed a drink of her martini.

"Maybe it's the way you check him out, Tab. Admit it, you want him."

"Drop the subject, Bri."

As soon as he reached the table, Nico grabbed the extra chair and sat down right next to Tabby. "What are we talking about, ladies?"

This had been the first time in months they actually looked at the menu and placed actual orders. Without Nico cooking tonight, things changed a bit. Kaylee watched as Luciano walked around the restaurant talking to the patrons, his movements as smooth and fluid as ever.

Did he ever get shaken up?

They were halfway through their meal by the time Luciano made another appearance at their table.

He looked so at home, so comfortable walking around his restaurant. He reminded her of a king in his palace. Confident, strong, familiar. Did people see her that way? *Bookends* was as close to a palace as she would ever get, as close as she wanted to get. Luciano obviously felt the same way.

"What do you think, Kaylee?" Tabby asked.

"What? I'm sorry I was just—" she tried to respond.

"Watching Luciano. We know." Bri laughed.

"I was not. What did you ask?" she dropped the Luciano subject like a hot iron.

"Nico invited us all out on his boat sometime in the next month or so," Tabby replied.

Kaylee could see her excitement. Tabby loved the ocean; she would live on it if she could.

Kaylee didn't know how to answer. In a month or so, she and Luciano would have ended their affair. No doubt he would be with Nico if they were all taking a trip out. Would it be weird to be around him after everything was said and done?

"It depends on what's going on at *Bookends*. Let me know when you have a date in mind." That was the best Kaylee could do.

"Girl, you need to take a break from your store once in a while," Bri replied. "If I can go, and I won't even have an Italian man on my arm like you and Tab, you can go."

"Who says I'll have an Italian man on my arm?" Kaylee asked irritated.

She felt overwhelmed. Everyone kept making assumptions about her and Luciano. It all bombarded her, and Kaylee didn't like it. She felt trapped and that scared her.

"I do," Bri replied.

"Ease up," Luciano said while pulling up a chair to sit next to Kaylee. "As far as anyone is concerned, Kaylee and I are friends. If there is anymore going on, it stays between us."

For the first time, Kaylee felt grateful that a man had come to her rescue. Luciano quieted everyone at the table with his tone. His voice could be strong and demanding when the situation called for it. Kaylee felt her resistance grow a bit weaker.

"Now I see why Nico calls you boss," Bri said with a smile. As the mood grew lighter everyone chuckled.

Kaylee sat at the table pushing her pasta around her plate with a fork. She was hungry but for some reason couldn't bring herself to eat. Not with Luciano so close by.

"Did you get tickets for the music festival?" Bri asked Tabby.

"They were already sold out," Tabby responded. "I wouldn't have been able to go anyway. I have an appointment with a client that day."

As Bri, Tabby, and eventually Nico continued discussing music; Kaylee sat quietly, consumed by Luciano's nearness. He hadn't said much since coming out and saving her. Here and there he made comments or answered questions, but didn't engage himself in the conversation like he usually did.

His eyes held a distant expression, but his body was uncomfortably close to her own. His leg ran the length of hers, brushing against her ever so slightly. The simple movements of his pants brushing against her bare skin was sinfully erotic. The heat threatened to burn her up. Thank God she'd worn a skirt tonight. His foot nudged hers and he continued to play with her under the table.

When his hand began the same gentle assault on her thigh she had to bite her lip. Though he wasn't touching her in the way her body craved, his fingertips seared her all the same. Feeling excited like she and Luciano were sharing a secret no one else knew.

He trailed a path of warmth up and down her leg, sliding ever so close to the wet, heat between her thighs, but never actually hitting the mark. Being brave, Kaylee glanced to the right catching the knowing, confident, grin on his face. He knew what he was doing to her, and he loved it. The evidence was written on his face, his smile, his eyes.

"Are you a big music fan, Kaylee" he asked ever so calmly.

"Mmm hmm," she replied her voice low.

Luciano's hand dipped between her thighs. Her panties were the only barrier between them. He might as well have touched her bare skin.

Turned on beyond belief, Kaylee leapt from her chair, her leg hitting the table, and not only her drink, but Nico's and Luciano's spilled on the table.

"What the hell?" Bri asked her eyes wide.

"Leg cramp," Kaylee groaned in response, knowing they didn't buy her excuse. "I'll be back. I need to go to the restroom." She needed a minute to compose herself, or hide. Hiding sounded like the better option.

Kaylee made it to the bathroom, locking the door before she leaned against the hard barrier. The bathroom was small and tidy. A rosy pink gracing the walls. *Damn him*, she thought. With one touch her resolve melted away, she felt primed and ready to go, and then reverted into klutz mode.

How did he do that to her? How would she ever get enough of that addictive touch? Kaylee moved to the sink ready to splash cold water on her face. Maybe that would wake her up from her ludicrous thoughts. Of course she would get enough of him. Soon, very soon, she'd get her fill and they'd both move on. She had to.

Moving her hand to the faucet, Kaylee heard a key turn in the bathroom lock. The door opened slowly. Luciano stood there blocking her.

"Ever heard of privacy? This is the second time you've barged in on me in the bathroom." She tried to sound annoyed, but knew she hadn't succeeded.

Luciano grabbed her hand and pulled her out of the bathroom. "Come with me."

Luciano's grip was tight as he practically dragged her down the hall. "Don't I have a choice?"

"There's always a choice, Bella. The look in your eyes indicated yours."

Of all the nerve! She couldn't bring herself to actually speak the words so she just followed. Luciano unlocked another door and led her to what she assumed to be his office.

"I want you," he said after he closed them inside. He backed Kaylee against the door. "Now!"

"You're getting a little bossy here, Luciano." Kaylee tried to sound strong.

"Tell me you don't want me," Luciano brushed his lips on her neck and flicking her left nipple through her top.

"I want you…" Luciano ate the rest of her words in a deep kiss. Shivers surged through her body. This man kept her on the verge just by being in his presence.

His kiss grew deeper and he lifted her. Surprise filled her as her legs wrapped around his waist on their own accord.

He was hot, hard, urgent as he leaned her against the door again, rubbing his erection against her heat. He felt so good; it hurt to say what she needed to say.

Pulling her lips away from his, Kaylee whispered, "But I can't have you."

"You're wet, Kaylee. You want me."

Confused, she struggled to make sense of tonight. First he acted like a jealous boyfriend, then he agreed with her, stating they were friends. He came out late but spent much more time with them tonight than usual, then he almost gave her the big O at their table. Her body wanted him, but her heart…no head, needed a break.

"Not now, Luciano. Brianna and Tab are waiting."

"They'll understand," he said kissing her neck again. "Nic will keep them company. I have to have you, Bella," he kissed her again, softly, his lips trailing up to her ear. "Right now."

She had been close to surrender before he uttered his last statement. Need. This wasn't about need. Even a sexual need. Want yes, need no.

Unwrapping her legs, Kaylee pushed Luciano away. "You're getting a little too pushy. I said not tonight." She knew her words were harsh but didn't care.

The desire all but disappeared from his almond shaped eyes. He looked serious, and sympathetic. "I would never push myself on you, Kaylee. I thought…"

"Shit," Kaylee mumbled walking over to sit in his black desk chair. "I know that. You know I want you too. Just not tonight. Can we leave it at that?"

"Yes, Bella, we can leave it like that."

Nico and Luciano were the only people left in the restaurant. The cleaning was done, the employees all gone, yet the men sat at one of the tables, drinking a beer, and eating garlic and herb bread sticks. Luciano sat sulking, and he knew it. At the moment he didn't give a damn.

Tilting back the icy cold, dark brown bottle, Luciano downed a mouth full. Condensation dripped down the bottle over his fingertips. The cool water nearly evaporated on his over-heated skin. After a couple hours, the thought of Kaylee still had him scorching hot.

"She's different," Nico said interfering with his thoughts.

Luciano didn't like to admit it but Nico had a way of knowing what went though his mind even when he didn't want to admit it to himself. "Yeah?" he replied.

"She makes you smile."

"Half the women in San Francisco make you smile, Nic, and I don't see you talking about how *different* they are."

"Lots of things make me smile, a good piece of pizza, flirting with a beautiful woman, cooking a great meal. Hell, I even make myself smile," Nico offered one to his cousin for good measure. "But we aren't talking about me, are we?"

Luciano pulled the tie from his hair letting it fall loose. He lifted his beer, draining whatever was left in the bottle. "You're starting to sound just like a woman, Nic. Lay off and hand me the other beer."

Nico handed the bottle over. "That, Lu, is because unlike you, I know just what women want. I've studied my craft well."

Luciano let out a roaring laugh. "You better study harder. You've been after Tabitha for how long now?"

Luciano saw his cousin flinch and realized he touched a soft spot without knowing it. The look vanished as quickly has it appeared. "Again, we aren't talking about me. We're talking about you and your woman." Nico said.

"I don't have a woman, I have a friend."

Luciano sat rigid in the chair, uncomfortable about where the direction of the conversation was headed. *It's just, Nic*, he told himself. *You've always been able to talk to him before.*

"I heard her spout a bunch of bull. Hell, she probably believes it just like you, but I know the truth."

"What, you're a mind reader now, too?"

"No, like I told you, I know women, and unfortunately for you, I know you, too."

Luciano frowned, something he was much more comfortable doing unless he was around Kaylee. "I'm thinking about ending it," Luciano said, surprised the words came out of his mouth.

Nico slammed his bottle on the table, "What?"

"Calm down, Nic. There's really nothing to end anyway. We agreed to enjoy each other's company for a while, and then call it quits. Maybe its time to make the call." He knew the words were true, but he didn't want to believe them. No matter what he told, Nico, Kaylee was different. She did make him smile, and he'd end up breaking her heart.

"So basically you're getting your jollies and then splitting?"

"That's been the plan all along. For both of us," Luciano took a frustrated breath. "Like you're any different?"

Nico gave him an irritated look.

"I know, I know, we aren't talking about you," Luciano said in response.

"Seriously, Lu, don't call it quits yet. Whether you want to admit it or not, you're feelin' this girl. I'm not saying it's time to start picking out china patterns or anything, but just go with the flow. See where it takes you."

Luciano downed the rest of his second beer. Nico's words penetrated his already weakened defenses. The only person he could come close to opening up to was Nico. "I already know where it will take me, Nic. That's the problem. Like I've always been told, I am my father's son."

The words felt wrong coming from his mouth. No matter that they were the truth. He didn't want to be his father's son, but he was. The fact that right now, at this moment, Kaylee did make him want to be different, was irrelevant. She *did* make him want more outside of his restaurant, she did make him want to have fun, to smile, to be free, but how long would it be until he ruined it?

"No, you're not, cousin. You never have been, and you never will be." Nico's voice sounded strained and serious.

"I'll never be able to give a woman all that she needs. Hell, it's after hours and I still can't leave this place."

"What about the other day? You jetted out of here when I told you I'd keep an eye on the place. Would your dad have ever done that?"

Luciano shook his head. Nico didn't understand, even *he* didn't know the whole story. "In the beginning? Yeah, he would have." Deciding to change the subject, Luciano said, "So, what about Tabby? You really like her or what?"

Nico sat for a few seconds, as if in deep thought before he answered. "I want her, I know that much. She's hot, and innocently sweet. I'd probably corrupt her or something."

"Sounds like *she's* different," Luciano replied.

"Naw," Nico scoffed. "I think it's just because she keeps shooting me down. A guy's pride can only take so much."

Nico was right. That had to be the reason he couldn't get Kaylee out of his mind too. Yeah, he knew she wanted him, but she didn't have time for him. With all the other relationships he'd had, the woman had been the one on the chase. He had always been the one being chased. A change like that would do a number on anyone's pride. Yeah, male pride. That's what it was, pure and simple.

Chapter Nine

Kaylee lay in bed, sleep just out of reach. Her body exhausted, yet her mind felt like running a marathon. After leaving *Luciano's* tonight all she wanted to do was put on a comfy, worn out pair of sweats, a t-shirt, crawl into bed and pass out. Why her brain didn't get that, she didn't know.

Well, maybe her brain did get it, but the pull Luciano had on her proved stronger. She couldn't get his dark eyes filled with desire out of her head. His look still held her, even though hours had passed. He wanted her...bad. The frightening part, she wanted him just as bad which is exactly why she had to pull away. Wanting too strongly could lead to needing, something she wouldn't let herself be capable of feeling.

The Daniels Curse. Granny Daniels had been cursed to lose her one true love at a young age, never to find another. Mama Daniels was a whole different story. She was a bum magnet and she "loved" them all. What was her curse? Was she a slave to her desire? She sure hoped not because she still desired Luciano and though she knew she would soon be forced to, she didn't want to give that up just yet.

Snuggling under her down comforter, Kaylee's mind raced. What would it feel like to really have a man jealous of her? Tonight, Luciano showed a façade of jealousy. Did she really want it to be real? *No, that would make things more difficult.*

She didn't need difficulty. Who did? Not with *Bookends.* She had a book signing coming up which made business great but her work load doubled. If things kept up this way she might need to hire help soon. She wasn't real fond of hiring someone to do what she knew she could do. Hard work energized her, fulfilled her, made her feel in control of her life.

No. She couldn't think like that. The only thing Luciano brought to her life was excitement. That's the only thing he would be allowed to bring to her life.

Kaylee glanced over at her clock with drooping eyelids. 2:15 AM.

Rolling over, she let herself succumb to sleep, her last thoughts were of Luciano.

Kaylee rushed around Bookends unpacking the boxes of books for the signing. The store looked a mess. Looked like she would be skipping her lunch hour today.

Ding, Ding. The bell over her door chimed. Kaylee looked up to greet her shopper to find Luciano. Her heart beat wildly in her chest. Did he come in for another lunch time rendezvous? Surveying the mess she knew that wasn't happening. Not today.

A gush of smoldering heat enveloped her. Why did he have to look so good? His hair lay loose teasing his neck. He wore a pair of black slacks, and a black shirt that hugged his muscled chest and arms. His eyes watched her as a frown formed on his kissable lips. Luciano didn't look happy to be here. Did he regret coming to see her?

The longer their eyes locked, the more Kaylee wanted him, and the more she forgot about her responsibilities at the store. She shuttered with the realization. After a few seconds, she realized Luciano shook as well. In fact, the whole store shook, books dropped from the shelves, pictures fell from the walls. Good God, an earthquake!

Luciano rushed to her side and wrapped his arms around her. She fought the urge to melt there.

"We have to stand in a doorjamb, Bella."

They made their way with books falling around them. The second they made it to their safe-haven, the earth stopped quaking. Luciano still held her in his arms, her curves molding along his harder angles.

For a split second, his closeness not only surrounded her body but crowded her mind, comforting her.

"Oh my God," she said looking around her store. "Look at my store." Kaylee pushed against Luciano trying to free herself from his strong hold. Books covered the floor, shelves stood empty, a few free standing bookcases were toppled over onto the floor.

"Let me go," she said still trying to escape him.

"Calm down first."

Kaylee took a few deep breaths feeling panicked. She knew she needed to calm down but couldn't. The state of her store had her mind reeling but she knew Luciano was right. She allowed him to hold her, to help her relax before trying to pull away again. "I'm relaxed. Can you please let me go now?"

He did as she asked and Kaylee headed straight for the mess. Plopping down on the floor in the middle of a pile of books. "What am I going to do, Luciano? I have a book signing tomorrow!"

Vulnerability laced her voice but she didn't have the strength to hold it back. She thrived on being prepared and now she was farther behind than before. Six authors and countless readers would be showing up at noon tomorrow. Feeling the tears prickle her eyes, Kaylee rubbed them with the back of her hand before looking up to see Luciano pace the floor. He had to be worried sick about his restaurant as well.

"Go ahead and go, Luciano. I know you need to get back to the restaurant."

"I'll be right back," was his reply as he headed out the front door, raising his cell phone to his ear. She watched him talk animatedly for a few minutes before he came back in and kneeled next to her grabbing a stack of books.

"What are you doing?" Kaylee asked.

"Helping you." Luciano stacked the books on a table next to the shelf, stood, and starting lifting the fallen bookshelf to its upright position.

the

Kaylee asked the question that floated through his own mind. What was he doing? Why was he staying here rather than going to check on the restaurant? *Nico said everything is fine.* He needed to be with Kaylee.

That damn vulnerability in her voice had done him in. Why, he didn't know. Maybe because he knew how hard it had to be for her. Luciano lifted a bookshelf right side up. Kaylee sat there watching him, disbelief on her face.

"Luciano?" she asked her voice obviously questioning.

"What?"

"You need to get back to your restaurant."

"Nico is there. He can handle it." Strangely he was okay with that. He wanted to be here for Kaylee.

"This isn't part of the arrangement, Luciano. I really don't need you. I can deal with this mess on my own."

He shook his head. "Damn the arrangement, Kaylee. This isn't about that. This is about a *friend* helping another *friend*. You did say we were friends, didn't you?"

"Yes, but—"

"No buts, Bella. I'm helping and that's that." Luciano grabbed a black rubber band out of his pocket, tying his hair back. "I know you don't need me." *Which is what you wanted, remember? It's what you need.*

"This could take awhile. I could just call Bri and Tabby to come and help me out."

"But you won't. Plus I'm here. I'm willing. I'm able. I might as well help." He was willing and able to do a lot when it came to Kaylee.

"Luciano—"

"Sh," Luciano walked over to her, knelt down and put his fingers against her soft lips, her chocolate skin beckoning him, begging for his caress. "The longer we argue, the more time we're wasting. We have a book signing to get ready for." Pulling her to her feet he didn't even let himself think about the fact that he'd just said *we*.

Kaylee felt dizzy, the familiar sensation she got when a wave of her Luciano induced klutziness might take over. To be safe she stood there not letting herself move. The books on the ground were a dangerous maze. She didn't need to feel more self conscience by reverting back to the Kaylee who couldn't walk, much less speak in front of the sexy Italian.

"Whatever floats your boat. If you'd rather help me out, I'm not about to turn it down," she tried to hide her uneasiness. She never expected this out of him. Would she do the same had she been at Luciano's when the earthquake interrupted their day? Probably not. No one would have been able to keep her away from her store.

"So, where do we start?"

"Let's get the overturned shelves back up. After that, I need to start going through the books. Getting them organized."

"What am I? Chopped liver?" he asked.

Kaylee looked at him clueless before saying, "What do you mean?"

"*We* need to start going through the books, Kaylee. Not you. When I do something, I do it all the way."

Yeah, didn't she know it? "Sorry," she replied. "I'm not used to having help around here," Kaylee said as they both walked towards another fallen bookshelf.

"You should. This is a lot for one person to do on their own. Working seven days a week is too much, Kaylee."

"Six."

"Yeah, right. I know you still work the only day of the week Bookends is closed."

Damn, she forgot about that. "Like you wouldn't do the same?" she asked.

"I've let Nico have a bit more responsibility lately. He's always wanted it anyway. To tell ya the truth, it doesn't feel half bad." Luciano knelt to lift the shelf. "I can do this part on my own, Bella."

"If you think that, you don't really know me, Luciano. This is my store. If I have to say we, so do you." Kaylee held a serious tone to her words.

"Deal," Luciano said waiting for her to take the other end before they effortlessly lifted the shelf.

They silently moved the last two shelves to their upright position. Kaylee watched him. Luciano raised his hands to his head, his elbows bent in a relaxed position as he returned her stare. His eyes swirling with a look she began to recognize.

"Don't look at me like that, Bella. We have work to do. I'd much rather enjoy you right now but I know how important this is to you."

He shouldn't have to remind her about that. She knew it and the knowledge didn't sit well. Would she have let him kiss her if he'd asked? Would she let herself forget about the store and let him make her feel good? Oh it was so tempting, but come tomorrow she'd regret it.

"I love the way you eat me up with your eyes, Kaylee. It's hard to ignore."

Heat swirled around them. How could this guy make her forget everything but him?

"What's next, boss?"

Kaylee smiled at Luciano calling her boss. "I'm beginning to realize you are a lot more like your cousin than you want to admit. Once you loosen up, I see a huge resemblance."

"You're kidding right? I love him but he's a huge pain in the ass. Are you calling me a pain in the ass, Kaylee?"

"You can be. Like right now, I know you should be at your restaurant, but you're here out of some weird obligation or something. And," she laughed again. "You just called me boss like he does to you."

He raised an eyebrow. "You know, I have no problem letting you be the boss once in a while. I'd love to sit back and let you run the show next time we—"

"Now look at you! Throwing out the flirtatious charm to cover up for yourself. You two are more like brothers than cousins. I don't know why I didn't notice it before."

"Nico's a great guy," Luciano said in a somber voice. "Much better than me. He may be a playful flirt, but he'll make a good husband and father one day. That's not in the cards for me."

Wow, where did that come from? It was meant to be a joke but Luciano sounded serious. Why didn't he think he would be a good husband or father?

Kaylee kept her mouth closed. She wanted to tell Luciano she thought he was a great man, and he would make a woman very happy one day, but she didn't let herself. She didn't want to think about him being another woman's, not ever.

Luciano saved her from saying anything. "Let's drop the subject okay?"

"Yea, okay," Kaylee replied.

"One last thing though, I'm not here due to any obligation. I'm here because it's where I want to be."

Kaylee walked over to the counter, then put on some music. As Tracy Chapman began to lightly flow through the small speakers, she showed Luciano where she'd like to begin with the books. Since tomorrow's signers were romance writers that was the section she wanted to start with. More than likely that would be where most of the business would come from.

Luciano got busy working hard beside her. Every now and again he'd pick up one of the books, making a wise crack remark about the cover or title, making her smile. It felt good to smile. The time fly by as they laughed and worked.

"Have you always loved reading?" he asked as they continued their task.

"Oh yeah," she replied. "Reading is an escape. When I needed to get away as a child, I'd crack open a book and get whisked away. I never stopped after that."

"Did you have a lot to escape from?"

When he asked the question, she knew she had said too much, opened up a little too much for comfort. "Just the usual," she replied.

"I hear ya."

He stared at her knowing she'd said a little more than she'd wanted to.

"So you turned your love of books into *Bookends*?" he continued the conversation.

"Well, first I had huge dreams of being a published author. That didn't work out too well for me. I have a couple of half finished manuscripts, but nothing good enough to submit."

"Now that surprises me." Luciano smiled.

"What?"

"The fact that you've left anything half finished."

"The rough drafts are actually finished, but they aren't any good. I didn't continue with them so technically they are still unfinished."

"How do you know they aren't any good?" his lips raised in a curious half smile.

"I can read."

Luciano picked up an older romance with a pirate carrying a

woman on the cover. He looked at it, shook his head and set it on the shelf. "Somehow, I think you're probably being harder on yourself than you need to be. You should pick them up again, show them to someone."

Kaylee thought for a minute before she replied. He seemed to have her pegged pretty well and that was uncomfortable. A wave of uneasiness washed over her body. "It's really not important. *Bookends* is my true love, anyway. Writing was just a hobby for me."

"You can have both, can't you?"

"Please. You've seen me. I run myself ragged just holding down the fort here. Can you imagine if I got back into my writing, too?"

"You could hire someone to help you here. You really need to do that anyway. You look exhausted."

"Yes, daddy," Kaylee teased. "Is that a nice way to tell me I look like crap?"

"Hell no," Luciano shook his head. "You're still hot, but you look worn out."

Kaylee perked up. Her body tingling from his compliment. "Thanks, I think," she smiled. "Today's just a hard day. I'm not usually as tired as I am right now. It's not everyday I face an earthquake."

"Have you thought about hiring any help here?"

Why is he so intent on me getting help at the store, she wondered?

"I've thought about it," she sighed. "You have to understand, *Bookends* is all I have. It would have to be someone I could trust completely."

"How often do you think you'd need help?"

"Not too much. For days like tomorrow with the book signing," Kaylee said finishing the shelf she worked on before moving to the next. "Book signing days are hard to do alone. I'm running back and forth between the register and the authors. I enjoy them though, and they're good for business. That's why I continue to do them."

"Is that all?"

"There are other times I could use a helper, but it wouldn't be more than a few hours per week. You are right though, I really do need to think about hiring someone."

Kaylee couldn't believe the words spilled from her mouth. She knew she did need help but that was the first time she made the commitment to get help out loud.

"What about you?" she continued. "It seems you've been leaving Nico in charge more often lately."

They sat in silence while she waited out Luciano's pause before he spoke.

"Nico's wanted more responsibility for a while now. I don't know why because his true love is being in the kitchen. But he's been trying to get me to give him more responsibilities."

"Maybe he's doing that more for you than himself," Kaylee said. "He probably sees you working so hard and know that you need to take a little time for yourself."

"How easy it is to point fingers when it's not you that we're talking about, Bella. The same thing could be said for you."

"But we aren't talking about me. I already had my turn." Kaylee laughed again letting herself enjoy their conversation. Even after an earthquake he'd been able to make her laugh. Somehow her stress eased as they worked together. She knew they'd finish. Something told her Luciano would be there all night if she wanted him to.

"You know what they say about paybacks, Bella."

"You're stalling."

"You're tough," Luciano rubbed his eyes with a frustrated hand. "I'm sure Nico thinks I should go out more, but he's wrong. I have my priorities straight with what's best for me. So, what time does the signing start tomorrow?" Luciano asked changing the subject.

Kaylee let the change come, part of her eager to learn more about Luciano, but fear that if they continued in that vein the tables would again turn and he'd be questioning her.

"Noon. I need to get the tables from the back and set them up in the open space over there," Kaylee pointed to a space in the front of the store. "I have the authors books still boxed up. Once I set them out I'm done for the night."

"I can help you do that too," Luciano said.

"Sure, that would be nice." The easiness of the words leaving her mouth again surprised her.

They talked a little while longer about hobbies, Bri, Tabby, Nico, and their work. He smiled a lot and that made her glad. Soon silence commenced while they continued the task of cleaning up her store. Every now and again, Kaylee stifled a yawn. She knew Luciano noticed but he didn't say a word. Who knew how much time passed before Luciano spoke again.

"You hungry, Bella? We need a break."

"Now that you mention it, I am a bit hungry. I haven't eaten since breakfast and didn't get much sleep last night. What time is it anyway?"

Luciano checked his silver wristwatch. "6:42," he replied.

"Are you serious? I can't believe we've been working for that long. I hate that I've had to keep my store closed all afternoon."

"We're not too far from being done with the clean-up. I think we can take a break for some dinner." Luciano pulled his cell phone from his pocket and dialed. "Hey Frankie. Are you guy's really busy right now? Good, can I talk with Nic for a second? Thanks."

Kaylee watched as Luciano held the phone to his ear. She wondered what he was up to.

"Hey Nic. Did Marco come in tonight?"

He sat there silent for a minute. As he sat there he started drumming his fingers on his knee. "Drop it, Nic."

He sounded angry. Kaylee wondered what Nico said to upset him so much. "Later," she heard Luciano say to Nico.

"Will it hurt you guys if Frankie makes a run down here? Good. Just something quick and easy. Thanks." Luciano closed his cell phone and slipped it back into his pocket.

"What was that all about?" Kaylee asked.

"I thought I'd get us something to eat."

"You know that's not what I meant, Luciano, but I'll let it drop. There are things I don't like to talk about either."

"You? No way?" Luciano kidded.

"Not funny," Kaylee picked up a magazine and tossed it at him. He caught it with ease.

"Hey, is that anyway to treat your product?"

"My product?" she said with a smile. "You and I have been sleeping together, but you're not my product. That's a pretty disrespectful way to look at yourself, isn't it?"

Luciano laughed. Not a soft, subtle laugh, but booming, contagious laughter that Kaylee couldn't help but catch.

"The magazine, woman." Sauntering towards her he continued, "Though I wouldn't mind being used by you, Kaylee. In fact, I think I'd rather enjoy it."

She backed up until the counter stopped her.

His predatory gaze following her like an animal on the hunt. Dangerous. She was the prey.

"I don't think so, mister," Kaylee teased. "We have work to do remember?" she dodged him, running behind the counter.

"We're on a break, remember?"

"To eat," Kaylee slipped out the opposite side of the counter.

"That can be arranged," Luciano countered. "You would be delicious."

Kaylee stumbled. Yep, she knew one of those piles of books would be the end of her tonight. She toppled over the stack, falling on her behind. She smiled a big toothy smile letting Luciano know she was okay without words. Right now, she didn't know if she would be able to speak.

"Cat got your tongue?" Luciano bent on the ground before her. "I'd much rather have it."

Luciano took her mouth in a consuming kiss. His tongue immediately tangled with hers. Kaylee leaned into him, her upper body pressed against his as she sat on the floor in a pile of books. He kissed her senseless. She forgot about the mess, forgot about the signing, forgot about the earthquake altogether as one of her own formed in her body.

Luciano eased his mouth away from hers taking with him his sweet, masculine taste.

"Can I taste you, sweet Kaylee?"

His voice wrapped around her, lulled her into an imaginary world where they could spend eternity in each others arms yet not risk her heart.

His face eased to the crook of her neck, his tongue sneaking out to lick her earlobe before drawing it into his mouth.

"Do I get an answer, Kaylee? Tell me yes. Tell me you'll finally let me take my time with you."

Unable to form words, a soft moan formed at the back of her throat and gained strength as it emerged her lips.

"I'll take that as a yes, Bell—"

A knock interrupted them.

"Shit," Luciano said pulling away from her. "Remind me again why I had the brilliant idea that we needed to eat?"

The moment broken, Kaylee slipped out from underneath him, scrambling to her feet, unlocking the glass door. Good God someone could have seen them! What had she been thinking? Oh wait, she hadn't been.

She opened the door to a young man with dark hair and a *Luciano's* Restaurant shirt on.

"I have a delivery for Luciano Valenti. Is this the right place?" he asked.

"I'm here, Frankie," Luciano said from behind her. The moment he was near, she felt the goose bumps bubble on her arms.

"Hey, Mr. V. Taking the night off?" the young man asked.

"Something like that," he replied taking the food and handing the teenager a twenty dollar bill.

"Thanks Mr. V! I better be getting back to work. Have a good one," he said turning and heading out the door. Kaylee locked up behind him.

"Well that was a mess," she said.

"That isn't the word I would have used for it."

"He could have seen us!"

"Kaylee, I'm not an animal. No one could have seen us at that angle.

We were on the ground behind a bookshelf."

Oh God, what's wrong with me? Why am I being so terrible to him? Unfortunately she knew the answer to that. She felt raw from their recent activities on her bookstore floor. They had fun, they laughed, and if Frankie wouldn't have come, she would have let him have her right there on the floor.

"It was just a little fun, Kaylee," Luciano said as if he knew what she thought. "If Frankie hadn't come, it would have been sex. Just like before."

Why did it hurt to hear him say that?

"I know that, Luciano. But I have a responsibility to this store, and I almost let that go to 'have a little fun'."

"We're taking care of your responsibility — You know what? Forget about it. Lets eat and get back to work."

Kaylee and Luciano moved to the couch, eating in silence. While she devoured her food, she felt her eyelids becoming heavy, begging for sleep. *Not much longer. We're almost done and then I can head up to bed.*

"I'll be right back," Luciano said his voice sounding distant.

As he walked away, Kaylee placed her plate on the table and leaned back on the couch to wait for Luciano. Her eyes closed to take a brief break while she waited.

Chapter 10

Luciano filled his hands with cold water before splashing it on his face. He needed a lot more than that to cool him off. His body was still turned on from his little game with Kaylee, and he was pissed. Horniness and anger produced a lot of heat in a man's body.

Why did she close herself off like that? They would have had sex, but they'd had sex before. Yet every time they did, or came close, Kaylee freaked as if she felt guilty. He had no experience with a woman like her. He wanted to stay as far away from a relationship as he could, but he couldn't keep his hands off her.

He knew she wanted him, but he had a feeling she didn't like that fact. But then, she only seemed to want him when he pushed her.

Since when did he become a bulldozer? Since when did he leave his store to get some?

Never.

She was seriously messing with his head and she probably didn't even know it. She had him spending time with her that he didn't really have. Time that would be better spent at Luciano's. That's what would be in his life forever, his restaurant, not the sexy woman with the braids that drove him crazy.

That's all she did. Drive him crazy. It wasn't anything more than that. He really should have listened to Nico and dated more. Maybe if it hadn't been so long since he got some, he wouldn't be so addicted to Kaylee. Maybe he wouldn't be sitting in the bathroom analyzing this like a woman. She made him want to break all his rules. Rules that were there for a reason.

No matter how much fun they might be having now, even if he and Kaylee were interested in trying to make it for the long haul, it would never work. Not with a son of Luciano Valenti. Not with a son who wasn't just the spitting image of his father but a compulsive workaholic.

Not now, man. Luciano grabbed a paper towel from the rack, drying his face and hands. Time to go back out and face temptation. It shouldn't be much longer and they'd be done. He made a decision to head over to *Luciano's* and get a little bit of his own work done tonight.

Opening the bathroom door, Luciano made his way back into the main part of the bookstore. Kaylee sat curled up against the couch, asleep. He stood there watching her for a minute. Her body relaxed and peaceful, something he didn't think she was when awake. God she was beautiful. Her hair pulled away from her face, a smile gracing her lips, lips he had to stop himself from kissing.

Making a quick decision, Luciano walked over to the counter, searching for her keys. He opened a cabinet under the register and found her purse, with a set of keys sitting next to them. Thank God. He knew better than to look in a woman's purse without her permission.

After grabbing the purse and keys he walked over to Kaylee and lifted her in his arms. To his surprise, she didn't wake. He hurried to the door, trying to walk fast and smooth as not to wake her. He had a lot of work left to do. After putting her to bed for the night, he had a bookstore to clean, and a book signing to prepare for.

Luciano tucked Kaylee into bed, the only sound a soft whimper as he laid her down. He snuck out of the apartment and headed back down to the bookstore. The clean-up didn't take as long as he thought. After he finished placing the last book on the shelf hoping he'd put everything where it should be he set up the tables for the signing.

Would she like it? Would she feel like he had taken over? All he wanted was for her to get some much needed rest. Luciano stood in the store a few seconds longer. The place looked really great. Luciano was feeling contented, not just about everything they'd accomplished today, but the whole setup. He could get used to helping Kaylee.

Grabbing the keys, he hit the lights and locked the door. Heading back upstairs, he placed the keys on the key rack by her door. He would have no way to lock the dead bolt, but at least he could lock the lock on the handle. Fighting the urge to go into her room, if only to watch her sleep, Luciano left her apartment. He didn't want to think about what he'd done tonight, about all the time he'd spent caring more about someone else's business than his own.

What's wrong with you, man?

Luciano jogged down the stairs intent on heading for his restaurant. He had *needed* to be there tonight. Needed to concentrate on his world for a while even if it meant not getting much sleep tonight. He had to get up early because there was a very important phone call he needed to make.

"Damn," Kaylee said jumping out of bed the next morning. She hadn't even set her alarm clock, yet her body automatically woke up on time. In fact, she didn't even remember going to bed. The last thing she remembered was eating, then closing her eyes for a brief rest on the couch. The next thing she knew she woke up after a restful night of sleep.

How could he let me fall asleep? Kaylee thought while pulling clothes from her dresser. She didn't care what she wore. The only thing she knew was she needed to get dressed and get down to the store ASAP so she could prepare for the signing.

Anger pulsed through her body. Why would Luciano carry her up to bed when he knew how much work she had to do? She planned to ask him that very question, after the signing. Right now, she had way too much work to get done, work she should have finished last night, work she would have finished if she hadn't messed around with Luciano and taken a break to eat.

Rushing to the bathroom, Kaylee washed up quickly, brushed her teeth, and threw her braids in a pile on top of her head. She hadn't even covered them last night! She pulled the black pants up and put on the snug yellow cotton shirt while walking down the hall. She grabbed her yellow flip-flops, slipping her feet into them before grabbing her keys. *At least he had the courtesy to put her keys where they belonged.* Even if he did overstep his bounds by bringing her up to her apartment without waking her up.

After locking the door, she hurried down to the store, prepared to walk in to the mess she'd left the night before.

"Oh...My...God!" The store looked amazing. All the books were off the floor. Walking through the isles, she noticed them neat and orderly. The real surprise came when she stepped foot in the open area in the front of the store. The tables were up, the books were out.

Did she do all this without remembering? She had been tired last night, but not that tired. No way would she not remember finishing the store last night. That meant only one thing. Luciano.

Her heart twittered. He had to have spent a few hours here after she'd fallen asleep. Most people would have used that as a reason to high-tail it out of there. Not Luciano. Why would he do all this for her? *Because he's a nice guy. Because he knew you needed help and needed sleep even more.*

The answer made it even harder for her to except. This was such a huge thing for him to do. It softened her defenses. That made his gesture more dangerous than anything.

Looking at the clock, Kaylee realized she had an hour until the store opened, three hours until the signing and nothing to do. Her body felt relaxed, but her mind felt restless. She needed something to do. *Bookends* was her life, her love, her responsibility.

Moving to the back, Kaylee grabbed the vacuum and her cleaning supplies. She had to do something. She traced the paths in the store three times with her vacuum before she started washing counters, straightening the backroom and cleaning the bathroom. The work helped but she still felt restless, useless.

The bell over the front door chimed five minutes after the store opened to a pretty woman with long dark hair. She looked familiar, like someone she knew, but Kaylee couldn't place where she would have met her before.

"Can I help you?" Kaylee asked.

"Are you Kaylee?" the young woman replied.

By the looks of her, she had to be a teenager, maybe her late teens but a teen all the same. How did she know her name?

"Yes, can I help you?"

"My name is Maria. I'm Nico's sister."

Kaylee's curiosity bubbled over. What was she doing here? Had something happened to one of them? If so, why would she come here to tell Kaylee?

"Nice to meet you."

"Luciano called me this morning. He said you might need some help today with a book signing. He knows I'm looking for a part time job. He promised me fifty dollars and told me to be here at ten."

Kaylee couldn't believe her ears.

"Don't worry. He didn't promise me anything beyond today," Maria said, probably reading the expression on Kaylee's face. "He just said you could use some help for today."

This just kept getting worse and worse. Luciano's kindness touched her in a way she didn't want to admit yet she also wished he'd asked her permission first. She needed to feel independent and though his help was probably the nicest thing anyone had ever done for her, it also made her feel like she was losing control. Not only of her store. Kaylee feared her heart might lose control as well.

"He told me to stop by *Luciano's* after I was done and he'd pay me."

Kaylee tried not to look appalled but knew she didn't succeed. After all he'd done for her today no way would she let him pay Maria as well. She should probably pay Luciano for his help too.

Maria laughed. "I wasn't supposed to tell you that part until later. He said you might freak out."

Kaylee smiled at the young girl's bluntness. She had a lot of her brother in her but that didn't matter right now. What mattered was Luciano and his crazy plans to pay someone who worked for her. Oh yeah, she was freaking out. Luciano had no idea how bad she was freaking out right now. He was crossing all kinds of her mental barriers yet for some reason she was letting him.

"Just so you know I'll be paying you today not Luciano. This store is my responsibility as are the employees." *Employees*? She wasn't sure if she planned to keep Maria working for her but she knew she needed the help for today.

Light shown in Maria's eyes. "You mean you're going to let me work?"

"Yes, I could use the help."

"Great! Where do I start?"

Kaylee showed Maria around the store, telling her what would be happening once the authors arrived. She wanted her to familiarize herself with the sections so she would be able to walk the store, helping customers during the signing. As Maria turned to do some exploring, she stopped looking over her shoulder and said, "Kaylee? Don't give Luciano too hard a time. It wasn't easy for him to come to me. You're the only girlfriend of his I've ever met. It must have really meant something to him that you had all the help you need today."

"But I'm not—"

"His girlfriend? I know. That's what he said to me too. Sorry, slip of the tongue."

Maria was older than her years. Luciano was not her boyfriend, but the young girl seemed to see more than Kaylee wanted her to.

"Remember what I said though," Maria added. "His heart's in the right place."

The walls around Kaylee's heart softened even more. Luciano really did go above and beyond to help. Not many people had ever done that for her. Her mom wouldn't have done if for her.

The day ran perfectly. Maria kicked butt! She stayed busy the whole time, helped Kaylee much more than she realized she could, and really seemed to enjoy herself. Luciano had done her a huge favor sending Maria in. Kaylee made sure to get her phone number. They decided that Maria would come in a couple times per week to help when she wasn't in school.

She was amazed at how much having an extra pair of hands helped her. With Maria, her main focus was college so the deal would be perfect for them. Kaylee would get the help she needed, on her terms, without feeling like she gave a big chunk of her own responsibilities to someone else, while Maria would get the extra money she needed for school.

Thank you, Luciano!

As soon as she cleaned up the store for the night, Kaylee locked up and headed straight for *Luciano's*. She needed to let him know that while she appreciated his gesture she needed him to talk to her before he made decisions about her store. As she walked up to the restaurant, Nico stood outside, his arms around a redhead, their lips locked.

She made sure to clear her throat as she walked by causing them to break away from each other. What a fool. If he ever planned to win Tab over, he'd have to get rid of all the women.

The girl walked away and Nico began to follow Kaylee inside. "Hot date?" she asked.

"I could ask you the same thing, babe. You and the boss getting together tonight?"

"No, we need to talk. Where'd your date go?"

"As you could tell, the date was over. I was just telling her good night."

"I thought you liked Tab?" Kaylee reminded him.

Nico winked. "I like all women, babe."

Kaylee swatted his arm. "God, being a jerk must run in your family! First Luciano, now you."

"What'd the boss do?"

"He sent your little sister over to help me work today, without my permission, and then he tried to pay her himself." Kaylee waited for Nico to agree with her.

"Of all the nerve!" Nico kidded. "I should take him out back and shoot him now. I can't believe he actually tried to do something nice for you."

With his words, she felt a bit foolish. Maybe she was overreacting a bit but Luciano had to know that her life was her own. He couldn't overstep his bounds. They had sex a couple of times, it was nothing more than that. *Yeah, right*.

Kaylee stood a few seconds before replying, trying to choose her words. The Italian seasonings permeated the air making her stomach growl.

"Did you eat?" Nico asked.

"What is with you guys always trying to feed someone?"

"We're Italian. It's what we do. We can forget the food for now though. What gives? Why are you mad at the boss for trying to help?"

"It's not that, Nico. I just... It's just... Never mind. I'm just confused. Do you know where he is?"

"In his office," Nico replied. "Go easy on him okay?"

For the second time today someone asked her to go easy on Luciano. Why? She doubted he would be the type to get his feelings hurt easily. He was a lot like her. He'd understand. Wouldn't he?

Kaylee started walking towards the office he'd kissed her in a couple weeks before.

"Hey," Nico called out. "I do like your friend but if you hadn't noticed, she keeps turning me down."

"You have to earn her, Valenti."

Luciano sat in his office doing some paperwork. The numbers all looked good. Business was picking up. When his dad left, Luciano's had been run into the ground. It took a lot of work to get it where it stood today. Luciano was proud of that fact. He put a lot of sweat into his business. His baby had finally began to grow into what he'd known she could be.

Did Kaylee feel the same way about her store? Of course she did. The woman seemed more obsessive than he did. Like right now, what even brought Kaylee to his mind? His thoughts had been on work and numbers, then there she was, filling his mind. He never let a woman get between him and his business before.

The only question, what to do about it?

Did he keep things going like they were? Fun, games and a little sex but nothing too serious. Did he cut things off with her completely before either of them got in over their head and ended up taking a risk and one of them getting hurt? No matter what they wanted, that would be the outcome. He knew he would never be able to make a suitable husband, not with his father's blood so strong in his veins.

He didn't even want to think about Kaylee. She barely made time for anything other than *Bookends*. The woman would run herself ragged in no time at all. So, why did he go through so much trouble for her? Why did he do whatever he could just to see her smile, to know she was happy? Why the hell couldn't he get her sexy body out of his head? Did he even want to?

A knock on the door stopped his train of thought.

Luciano stood up, ready to go back to work, assuming one of his employees stood behind the door. Opening it quickly, he got a surprise.

Walking in the door and closing it behind her, Kaylee said, "What were you thinking carrying me up to my bed last night without waking me up?"

"I had to finish with the store," Luciano winked. "I didn't realize you'd want me to wake you up for a little action before I went back downstairs."

No, no, no. She would not let him turn this into a joke. "You know that isn't what I meant! You shouldn't have done the clean up by your-self. *Bookends* is my store and you took over."

"Is that what you think?"

No, but it's easier for me to show you anger than gratitude. "It's what you did. Not only by finishing all the cleaning but by sending Maria over as well. You just assumed I'd need the help and you took the responsibility of sending someone over, not giving me the opportuni-ty to say no if I wanted to."

"You did need help. You said so yourself," his voice wavered with an angry tone. "I knew you'd never actually ask someone for help though."

"That's not the point, Luciano. I can't handle someone interfering in my life like that. I'm sorry but I can't." *It's too close to the intimacy I'm trying to avoid with you.*

Luciano stood there a moment, silent. Thinking? Angry? Kaylee watched, waiting for him to respond.

"I helped a friend out. That's all. Your life is your own, Bella. We don't have that kind of relationship."

His words held their truth but they stung nevertheless. They were getting too close. It became painfully obvious by the pain she felt in her chest. Kaylee pushed her pain as far away from the surface as she could. "I know that!"

"Don't worry. It won't happen again."

The look in his eyes helped the words flow from her mouth. "I know you meant well. Thank you."

Kaylee wondered why he feared the same intimacy that strangled her with terror but she didn't ask. Couldn't ask. Finding the answer would be too personal.

"What kind of relationship do we have, Bella?"

"Sex," she replied as much to remind herself as well as to answer his question. She had struggled to keep her anger about the store. It would be so easy to begin to fall for him but what would be the point? In the end, the outcome would be the same. True love didn't exist.

"Yes, sex, Bella." Luciano began to kiss her neck, his hands firmly planted in her thick braids. "Friends with benefits."

"Wanna cash in some benefits?" Kaylee asked urgently before she attacked his mouth in a fierce kiss.

He backed her against his desk, his fingers moving down to the but-tons on her pants. She needed this. It helped to remind her where they stood, what they were about, enjoying each other sexually, nothing more. It couldn't be anything more. No matter what she might want to believe. For Kaylee, this was it.

"You can't imagine how much I want you right now," Luciano's words pierced her thoughts as his hands pulled at her pants. When he got them to her knees, Kaylee finished the job for him pulling her legs out one by one. Luckily her panties went down with them so they didn't have another barrier between them.

Her body sizzled under his touch as Luciano pushed her shirt off her shoulders and undid the front clasp of her bra. He didn't bother to take them off completely. The mood was too urgent, too burning to take the extra time. Her body oozed with not only sexual excitement but the knowledge they were doing something they shouldn't. Not in the middle of his office while his restaurant was packed.

At the moment she was a rebel, a bad girl and the idea urged her on more.

The second Luciano's mouth clamped onto her aching nipple all other thoughts ceased to exist. She had to bite her tongue to keep from crying out. Kaylee wrestled with the button on his pants. She ripped down the zipper to free his erection. Fumbling, she finally lowered his pants and boxer briefs just low enough so she could grasp his shaft.

Running her hand up and down every hard, hot inch of his length, Kaylee savored the feeling of Luciano's mouth as he moved to her other breast.

"You're playing with fire. Keep that up and I'll be finished before we really get started."

Kaylee didn't want to wait any longer. Her body called out for Luciano to fill her, fast, hard, and now. "Then I guess we better get started."

He growled in her ear before pulling his wallet out to retrieve a condom. Sheathing his erection in seconds he filled her body in a quick, strong thrust.

They moaned in unison before Luciano started pounding away just the way she needed him to. As his body slammed in and out of hers Kaylee dug her teeth into his shoulder to keep from calling out. The pleasure was too great, too intense. With one swift thrust from Luciano, Kaylee came, a scream almost erupting from her body.

Chapter Eleven

The next few weeks went by in a whirlwind. *Bookends* boomed with business which Kaylee couldn't be happier about. Maria turned out to be an excellent asset. She worked a couple days a week helping Kaylee in every way imaginable. They talked a lot, Maria always questioning her relationship with Luciano, Kaylee always insisting they were just friends. She left out the, 'with benefits part.'

Lately, she didn't even know if they qualified as friends. Since their last erotic adventure in his office, they hardly had time to talk. The past two Friday's at Luciano's seemed tense. It was hard to tell if it was her doing or Luciano's but she found that she missed talking with him. She missed his smiles, his laughs, their conversations, she just plain missed her friend.

When had they forged such a strong friendship? A couple months ago, she couldn't speak around the guy, even though they saw each other once a week. As they'd spent more time together, she'd realized what a great person he really was and, beyond being an incredible lover he also cared like no other man she had ever known.

She missed Luciano. Missing someone opened your heart for the possibility for hurt, something Kaylee's heart fought widely against. It couldn't stand any more hurt. Just the thought paralyzed her, froze her already hardened barriers. The fear made her stay away, the time apart made her miss him more.

What am I doing? I need to forget about him, cut off ties before it's too late. So why couldn't she stop thinking about him? Today she wanted to ask Maria about him, but she didn't. Holding her tongue proved almost an impossible task.

It took double the time it should have for Kaylee to finish her inventory. Every time she'd get into a groove, Luciano popped into her head. Their last sexcapade in his office was never far from her thoughts. It had been wild, crazy and exciting. He'd started a fire she was far from dousing.

It had been good, but different. Different than any of the other times they'd had sex. In his office that day she'd felt like she needed him for the first time. The word need didn't belong in her vocabulary. She didn't want to need anyone but she couldn't stop thinking about him.

"I can't keep doing this," Kaylee spoke out loud to herself not caring if anyone walked in and heard her. She wanted to see him. Should she? What could it hurt to keep spending time with him like they had been? So far things seemed to be going well. As long as she didn't let herself fall in love with him, it couldn't hurt to continue to enjoy his company. It'd actually feel pretty good to enjoy him.

I always take things too seriously. How many times had Bri and even Tabby told her that? Way too many times to count. Finally making up her mind, Kaylee picked up the phone. The plan was to loosen up all along. Why change it now? Why start looking for something that wasn't there? Why start reading something into nothing? *Because it gives me an excuse to run.* Well not anymore. She planned to enjoy their affair for as long as it lasted.

Kaylee dialed the phone in triumph, proud of herself. She could keep Luciano at arms length and still have fun with him.

"Thank you for calling *Luciano's*. How can I help you?"

"Hi. This is Kaylee Daniels. Is Luciano available?" There, that was easy.

"Hold on one moment please," he hostess said. Kaylee felt her heart rate accelerate slightly but she took a few deep breaths to calm herself.

"Hello?" came Luciano's voice, smooth as butter.

How'd he do that? Kaylee tried for the same nonchalant manner by saying, "Hey, what's up?"

"Just working. How about you?"

Kaylee heard the smile in his voice. "I can let you go if you're busy."

"I don't think so, Bella. I believe this is the first time you've ever called me. I'm wondering what's going on."

You can do this. "Well, I was thinking maybe we could get together. We haven't really talked much since…"

"Yeah, it's been awhile. And when you're…you haven't really been there lately."

Oops. Looks like Luciano didn't let things go too easily. "Look, I'm sor—"

"Don't say it," Luciano demanded. "Don't apologize. It's over and done. We each learned something from it."

He sounded detached, something she hadn't heard in his voice before. Had she ruined it? Was the affair over?

"I have a large birthday party coming in tonight. I can't get away," he continued.

Yep, it's over. Probably for the best anyway, Kaylee thought. "Oh, I see."

"But, what do you say about this Friday?"

Friday? Another quickie in his office wasn't what Kaylee had in mind.

"Sure, you want to meet between drinks and dinner or what?" Why did her voice come out sounding so angry? She felt the ice dripping from her own words. They were cold and more detached than his earlier.

"Actually, that's not what I meant at all. I bought a couple of tickets to the music festival a few weeks back. I thought maybe you'd like to go. I know you and your friend were thinking about going but the tickets had been sold out. I got lucky and found a couple on eBay."

Like a date? No, no. She wasn't ready for this. Sure they went out that first time, but that was weeks ago. They hadn't gone anyplace together since. For some reason it seemed different now. *What happened to loosening up and having fun? Its not like the guy proposed marriage or anything.* She'd wanted to enjoy him so this would be her chance.

"What time does it start?" she asked.

"Three o'clock. We'll both have to take the afternoon off and—".

"I can't close my store!"

"What about Maria. She helps you on Fridays doesn't she? I'm sure she could handle it, Kaylee."

She had no doubt Maria could handle it. Her only doubt was herself. Could she handle it? "I don't know."

"I just thought it would be something different to do. I bought the tickets awhile back. I know you, Brianna and Tabby wanted to go and couldn't. I didn't want you to miss it too so I went on eBay."

He'd bought the tickets for her? Her skin tingled at the thought. And she really did want to go. *Badly*. She and the girls had been trying to go for a few years now but never were able to make it. Now she had the chance. Without thinking Kaylee opened her mouth and said, "Yes."

Luciano sat in his black leather chair, shocked. Shocked Kaylee called him, shocked he asked her to the festival, and shocked she said yes. When he bought the tickets he did have the intention of inviting her. Why, he didn't know. He knew he'd beat himself up later for missing the time at work, he knew it was a mistake but he couldn't stop his finger from clicking the button to buy the damn tickets.

Then she brought everything to light when she'd come into his office pissed as all hell. He'd been angry at first but she'd had every right to be mad at him. He did overstep his bounds. How would he have felt if she had taken over at *Luciano's* sending in help without his permission. He knew he'd be furious. In fact, he'd probably run for the hills. That kind of help came from someone you really cared about, someone who meant more to you than friends with benefits. Kaylee couldn't be more than that to him.

The why of it all is what bothered him the most. Why did he need to help her so much? Why did he want so much to do anything to make her life easier while ignoring his own? He drove a dangerous road and knew it. He would end up hurting her. No matter what, he could never give her what she deserved so he thought it best to cut his ties. He'd kept himself as far away as he could. He hadn't called her, had tried not to think of her. In essence he'd moved on with his life.

Then she'd called him.

For the first time.

All his work came crashing down. He missed her. That feeling pushed the invitation to the concert from his mouth. An invitation that before her phone call he'd decided not to make. Too late now. He'd have to make the best of it, not that it would be very hard.

***

"I can't believe you're ditching us tonight," Bri said to Kaylee.

"I can't believe the two of you are standing in my store at 10:00 AM. Don't you have jobs to go to?" Kaylee replied.

"Personally, I'm happy for you, Kay," Tabby added. "I think it's great you and Luciano are spending some time together. Are you getting serious?"

Kaylee flinched at her words. Tabby never learned. "Do you even know me? Girl, you must be crazy if you think I'm getting serious with any man. You know how I feel about that." Kaylee sat down on the couch by the register at *Bookends*. "I'm just nervous about leaving my store today."

"Would you forget about the store? You're spending the day with a gorgeous man. You're going to be relaxing outside listening to music half the day then you'll come home and have mind blowing sex. The store is the last thing that should be on your mind." Brianna held a serious tone to her slightly playful words.

"You trust Maria, right?" Tabby added.

"Yea, I do. She's a great kid. I have no doubts she'll do fine. It's more me I'm worried about." Kaylee shook her head. "You know what? Forget I said that. The whole point is for me to have fun and that's what I plan to do. I'm really tired of over-thinking every little thing."

"You go girl," Brianna added giving her friend a high five. "That's what I like to hear." Then she turned to Tabby, "Now if I could get you to go out with his cousin we'd be in business. Both of you would finally be getting some."

"Nico's pretty tied up, I think. I saw him making out with some redhead a few weeks back," Kaylee told them.

"So," Bri said.

At the same time Tabby looked shocked and maybe a little bit hurt when she said, "Good. I hope they'll be very happy together." The words didn't ring true as they left her lips. For the first time Kaylee really wondered if her friend had more feelings than she was willing to admit for Nico. She hated to be the one to tell her that he'd been spotted with another woman but figured it for the best. He wouldn't mean it but he'd be nothing but heartache for Tabby.

Kaylee paced the floor, her palms sweating, nervousness suffocating her. Forcing her fears down, she turned to Maria. "Here are the keys. Make sure you don't forget to lock up when you leave. Go ahead and take the keys with you. They're my spare. Just make sure you don't forget to bring them back to me tomorrow when you come in. Hopefully we won't be too busy tonight. If so, I have Tabby's number by the phone. She can help you out if there's any kind of emergency. You have my cell number, right?"

"Kaylee. Calm down. It'll be alright. I swear you look like you're about to pass out or something," Maria smiled. "Have a good time tonight. I'm so happy you and Luciano are seeing more of each other."

"It's not what you think, Maria."

"Well whatever it is, keep it up. Nico says you're good for Lu. He deserves that."

Kaylee didn't know what to think about that. Nico talked about her and Luciano to their family? He thought she was good for him? *What am I thinking*? Who cares what Nico thinks? She and Luciano weren't anything to each other, except for friends, something she realized they really were.

"Maria, we're only-"

"Friends. I know. Have fun anyway, will ya? You both need it."

Kaylee needed to have fun. Maria stood in front of her and Kaylee knew what the young girl said held true. "Yea, I'll have fun. Just make sure—" The bell over the door rang. Luciano stood in the doorway looking sinfully sexy. His hair hung loose around his shoulders just the way she liked it. He looked comfortable in a pair of khaki shorts and a dark blue polo shirt.

Thank God she went causal as well wearing a pair of blue shorts, a white tank top, and flip-flops to match. She would have fun today. She'd make sure of it.

"You aren't having second thoughts are you, Bella?" Luciano asked.

Kaylee wasn't apprehensive, not now. Right now her body felt primed for a good time. Primed for Luciano. Someplace in the background, Kaylee heard Maria laugh.

"What are you laughing at, Maria?"

"Oh, nothing," Maria smiled. "Just anxious for you two 'friends' to have fun today."

Kaylee finally made herself speak. "Naw, not apprehensive. Just ready to get out of here."

Kaylee and Luciano stepped outside into a perfect spring day. A light breeze tickling her body as they walked down the hilly street to Luciano's car. People walked about, holding hands, chatting, and window shopping on the streets.

The city was alive with culture. A man with long black dreads sat on the street corner playing his guitar and singing a reggae beat while a group of tourists circled him, clapping. The city looked so much more alive today. The sun seemed to shine extra bright, the smiles on the faces of the occasional passersby showed a bit more teeth. Kaylee took in the surroundings like a tourist herself, determined to see things differently today, determined to have fun and enjoy herself like never before.

When Luciano reached out to grab her hand heat surged up her arm landing incredibly close to her heart.

"I'm glad you decided to come today."

He stood so close, his body melding along hers. His thumb began making circles on her hand. She stared at his olive colored fingers intertwined with her own rich, dark brown skin. Their hands contrasted in every way. One dark, one lighter. His large and rough despite the fact that he worked indoors. Her own, smaller and more delicate. Had she ever seen anything so beautiful as their hands entwined?

Unable to form words, Kaylee looked up at Luciano hoping her eyes conveyed what she needed to say.

"Can we make a deal?" he finally asked.

"What kind of deal?"

"Today is only today. You and I both know what the future holds for us." Luciano exhaled a breath. When he spoke again his words held a slightly shaky tone. "Let's have fun, Kaylee. We won't worry about tomorrow. We won't worry about the restaurant or your bookstore. Today we worry about having fun and leaving everything else for tomorrow."

Somehow it felt as though he'd plucked the thoughts from her brain. This was their last day together, their last day to enjoy one another before they said goodbye. God she didn't want to think about tomorrow. Luciano was right. They needed today because after that there would be no more days like it.

Chapter Twelve

"**H**ave you ever been to the Great Meadow before?" Luciano asked as he merged onto the freeway.

"No. I hear it's beautiful though."

"It is. I won't tell you about it. I want to watch you experience it with virgin eyes."

Kaylee popped him on the leg with her hand. "Then why'd you bring it up?"

"So I could torture you." Then getting more serious he said, "These last couple weeks have been torture for me, you know? I've craved getting that hot body of yours naked."

Kaylee laughed. "So now you want to torment me? Let me tell you, I've been pretty crazed myself these past couple weeks."

"Do you plan on relieving that tension tonight?"

"You know what?" she asked. "I've missed the Italian Stud. I think I'd like to give him another try tonight." *Good God, did I really just say that?*

Luciano took his eyes off the road to look at her. "I think that can be arranged, Bella. How long is this concert anyway?"

"You are so bad. I think you can hold off for a few hours. Keep your eyes on the road. I want to get there in one piece."

Kaylee and Luciano chatted while they made the drive to The Great Meadow. What in reality was a thirty minute drive, felt like an eternity. Soon enough they pulled into a parking spot and Kaylee jumped out of the car.

"I've always wanted to come to one of the music festivals up here," she said smiling.

Luciano opened his trunk and pulled out a black duffel bag. "I brought supplies. You'll see when we get situated."

As they walked, Luciano reached out again grabbing her hand. *How strange*, Kaylee thought, *Luciano is the first man I've ever walked hand and hand with*. Not many twenty-eight year old women could say that. Sure she'd probably held some guy's hand in high school but never as an adult. She'd never walked down the street holding a lover's hand. *How did holding hands with Luciano feel more intimate than having sex with other men?*

As they made their way up the hill to the large grassy area Kaylee stopped in her tracks. In the distance you could see the Golden Gate Bridge in all its glory, the water stretched out below. The air felt crisp and clean. Trees and flowers graced the lawn sporadically. Jazz music filled the air.

"You're right. It is beautiful." The words came out on a deep soul cleansing breath.

"I'm glad you like it," he said dropping a light kiss on her forehead. "Let's sit down before it gets too packed."

She didn't want to leave that spot but she did as Luciano said. They sat on the outskirts of the crowd making their own more private retreat. He opened the bag and pulled out a red and white checkered blanket. It reminded her of the table cloths you found in some Italian restaurants. He then pulled out a small basket that obviously held food.

Wow he had come much better prepared than she had. *This is a first.* She usually made sure to be prepared for everything.

"Are you hungry now or do you want to wait?" he asked.

"I'd rather wait." Kaylee grabbed the blanket and spread it on the ground before sitting down. Luciano followed, setting the basket and the bag next to them.

As the soft saxophone played in the background, Kaylee smiled at Luciano. She felt happy. *Have I ever felt like this before?* If so, she couldn't remember.

Sitting there watching Luciano she wished her luck were different. Wished she could risk falling in love. Sadly, she knew that would never be. Luciano winked like he knew what went though her mind. *Today isn't about the what if's*, she reminded herself. As Luciano caressed her cheek, Kaylee smiled. "Thank you." He knew her better than most people. He knew this wasn't the time for words.

Luciano's heart pulsed in his chest like it never had before at the look on Kaylee's face as the soft thank you escaped her lips. Whatever he did right today, he wanted to keep on doing it. Everyday, all the time, but he knew he couldn't. He just wasn't made that way. Not for the long haul at least.

As he moved behind her, pulling her to sit between his legs, her back aligned with his chest, he wished like hell it was possible. For now he held her tight, trying to hold onto the moment. Could she feel his heart beating wildly against her back? In some ways, he wished she did. Wished she could know without words how she affected him, how she made him feel. He would never tell her, couldn't risk it.

So he held her. Let the sounds of the music lull them, speak to them. From the sounds of the sax, to the piano, and the smooth guitar, it all seemed to be playing just for them.

Kaylee sat in Luciano's arms listening to the music, reveling in what it must feel like for couples in love. If this is how it felt, she'd really missed out on more than she realized before. Trying to hold onto the feeling as long as possible, she sat in Luciano's arms afraid to move.

Her rear end ached from being in the same position, her legs felt cramped but sill she didn't want to move.

"Are you getting hungry?" Luciano whispered into her ear.

For you, she thought. Ignoring the words in her head, Kaylee replied. "I could eat. How about you?"

"I'm Italian," Luciano kidded. "I can always eat."

Kaylee felt the immediate absence as Luciano sat her up and moved away to grab the food. The warmth of his body left her feeling cold despite the warm sun shining above. Luciano pulled a small lunch bag out with Italian pasta salad inside. He handed her a bowl before grabbing his own. They ate in silence, the music keeping the silence comfortable.

"That tasted great, Luciano. Thanks for thinking ahead. That's usually my job."

"I own a restaurant so food is pretty easy for me to come by." Luciano smiled.

After the meal they returned their attention to the stage just as India Arie began her set. As her graceful voice began to sing, Kaylee rocked back and forth letting the music ease into her soul. Her eyes drifted closed without her knowledge as she let the tune continue to relax her.

Forgetting her surroundings she lost herself in the sounds around her.

"My God you're beautiful." Luciano's voice spoke low and husky.

Feeling slightly embarrassed Kaylee turned to look at him. "I love her music. Sometimes I forget everything when I'm listening to it."

"I can see that. I wish I hadn't interrupted you."

"I've thought about adding a small music section in *Bookends*. Maybe where people can exchange old CD's for new ones. Something like that."

"You should do it."

"Books and music. I couldn't live without them."

"What else couldn't you live without, Bella?"

Kaylee sat in thought a few seconds. The only things important in her life were her store, Bri, and Tabby. How sad. She had no close family, only two close friends, and her job. Should there be more to life than that? "Nothing. Is that sad or what?"

"I'm sure there's more. You just haven't admitted it to yourself." Luciano's eyes spoke stronger than his words. Somehow she thought there was something he needed, something he wouldn't allow himself to need.

"What about you?"

"My restaurant. My family. My mom's great and Nico's family has always been there for me too." He spoke to her but looked into the crowd, towards the stage, anyplace but her eyes.

"What about your dad?" Kaylee saw his fist clinch. "You don't have to tell me. I shouldn't have asked."

"No. It's okay. You should know anyway. I'm so damn much like my dad you deserve to know."

Kaylee sat quietly watching India singing her beautiful song in the background. She couldn't believe Luciano was opening up to her, talking to her about something that obviously hurt him. It touched her heart. He touched her heart.

"From what my mom said my parents used to be happy once. But everything changed after I was born. She said they used to do everything together. Concerts, vacations, walks in the park, anything to spend time together. They worked at a little Pizzeria together, didn't take life too seriously. You know that kind of thing."

Surprise filled Kaylee's mind. Why was he sharing this?

"They lived in the moment, didn't make any big plans. Then my mom got pregnant with me. Right after they found out they married. Even though it wasn't planned she said she couldn't have been happier. About me and about the marriage." Luciano paused.

"And your dad?" she asked.

"I guess he just liked their life the way it was. He knew he'd need a better job, knew my mom would have to stop working, knew things would change. My mom said he bought the restaurant trying to make a better life for us. Soon it consumed him and that's all he thought about."

"So he worked a lot?" Gee, that sounded familiar.

"He worked all the time, Bella. He worked seven days a week, never made it to my school functions or my games as a kid. The only reason he made it to anyone's birthday is because they were always celebrated at *Luciano's*. Nico's dad is the closest thing I ever had to a father. When I graduated high school he actually made it to my graduation. He just never made it home afterwards. We haven't seen him since."

Oh my God! "I'm so sorry." Her heart ached for him. She hated the pain that he'd seen. Hated that she couldn't take it away for him.

"Don't be." He sounded harsh, closed off. "My dad ran *Luciano's* into the ground towards the end. He stopped putting money into the place. Hell, he probably stocked up for his escape. We had to close the place for awhile. After I got my business degree we opened the restaurant back up." Luciano stroked her cheek. "Aren't you sorry you asked about my dad?"

"I'm sorry you had to deal with that but I'm not sorry I asked. I just don't understand why you shared it with me."

"I inherited more from my dad than his name, Kaylee. Even as a child I was an overachiever. When I set my mind to something, that's it. Nothing else is important. I'm just like him, a workaholic with no time for anyone."

"I think you're wrong there. Look at how you helped me after the earthquake. For some reason you cared more about my store than your restaurant."

The sun started to set and a cool breeze brushed over them. Luciano reached into his bag and pulled out another blanket. He moved to sit behind Kaylee again, pulling her close and wrapping the blanket around them.

"That was a fluke. I beat myself up over it later, felt guilty about it. My whole childhood people compared me to my dad, Bella. Our looks, our personalities, our workaholic nature. The thing is he wasn't always that way. In the beginning he doted on my mom. After I came and *Luciano's* opened, he forgot about her. You know how affectionate Italians are, right?"

"Yes."

"You know I don't ever remember seeing my dad hug or kiss my mom? I can tell you he damn sure never did it to me."

"I'm so sorry," she said again. The words seemed so empty but she didn't know what else to say. Part of her yearned to open up to him the way he did to her, but she couldn't. Couldn't share those painful memories.

"I can't risk ever hurting a woman the way my dad hurt my mom."

"I think you're too hard on yourself." *Am I too hard on myself as well*?

Luciano bent his head and began placing soft kisses to her neck. His lips tickled her skin softly like the breeze blowing across her face.

"I made you miss your favorite singer," he whispered.

Kaylee looked up to see the next performers on the stage. Her mind and heart were so engrossed in Luciano, so wrapped up in his world she hadn't even noticed.

"That's okay. I like talking to you. I like learning more about you." Kaylee tilted her head away from him giving him better access to her neck.

"I don't understand it," he said against her skin. "But I'm glad I could make you understand the kind of man I am."

She pushed away from him. "Are you crazy? That story broke my heart but it doesn't tell me anything about the man you are, Luciano. The fact that you brought me here, tells me who you are. That you stayed and helped me with my store when you didn't have to. Those are the things that make you the man you are. If I didn't already know how it would turn out for me, if all the women in my family didn't have such bad luck with men, I just might have fallen in love with you."

Kaylee's words should have sent him packing, hiking back up the hill as fast as he could to bring her home and get the hell away, but they didn't. Just the opposite. They made his heart swell. Made him wish things could be different.

"Oh, God. I shouldn't have said that." *Love? Where the hell did that come from?* "I didn't mean it. Well, I meant the part about you being a great guy, but I didn't mean the falling in... well you know. I didn't mean that part. I don't do love. Never have, never will." *Shut up and quit rambling.*

Luciano leaned forward to quiet her with his mouth. He kissed her crazy, kissed her senseless, kissed her into forgetting her words. Their tongues intertwined, exploring what now was familiar. He knew all the dips, curves and corners of her addictive mouth.

Today. Focus on today. Don't worry about tomorrow.

Luciano moved his hand and buried it in her hair, grasping her head to pull her closer. He felt her leaning in too, her body raising to sit on her knees, her hands moving to each side of his body.

"Damn," Kaylee said pulling away and shaking off her right hand. She'd put her hand right in one of the bowls of food. Pasta and black olives sticking to her fingers.

"Looks like I pulled another Kaylee," she laughed.

The mood suddenly lightened which he needed. Things were too intense, he'd shared too much, much more than he'd ever shared with any woman before.

"It's been a while since the last time though. You have to admit I'm getting much better."

"Impossible," Luciano said. "You can't get any better than you already are."

After Kaylee cleaned up her mess they started to pack away the supplies. The concert was coming to a close soon. Couples started to leave probably trying to avoid traffic. Luciano suggested they do the same. While packing away the blankets, closing the food containers, and organizing it all to fit in the duffel, Kaylee and Luciano talked almost non-stop.

They didn't discuss anything serious. After the way they spent part of the afternoon, she had the feeling they both needed light conversation. The supplies where packed and before she knew it they were in his car driving back towards her place.

As they merged onto the freeway a thought struck her. Kaylee hadn't thought about *Bookends* all day. She didn't even miss her store.

Wow, how weird. Not able to remember the last time she felt like this, Kaylee shook her head before turning to look out the window, watching the cars race by. *My store should be the most important thing in my life yet I feel great having neglected it all day?* That didn't sit well. Her stomach churned uneasily.

"Don't even think about—," Luciano said from the driver seat.

Kaylee looked at him in surprise. "Don't think about what?"

"I see that far off expression in your eyes. You realized how much fun you had today and you're letting yourself feel guilty. You start that up and I'm liable to do the same thing."

When did he get to know her so well? How could he read her thoughts just by an expression on her face or a far off look in her eyes? *Today. Focus on today.*

She turned to watch as Luciano gripped the steering wheel. "When we get to my place, will you come up?"

"Yes."

"Good. Now get your eyes back on the road before you get us killed."

Luciano smiled and Kaylee couldn't help but do the same.

Since it was late evening he found a parking place right in front of the store. Opening the door, Kaylee stepped onto the sidewalk fighting the urge to head straight into the store. From the outside, things seemed perfect, but she so wanted to go inside just to make sure. Some habits were hard to kill.

"Let's go inside first, Bella. We'll check out the store before we go upstairs."

He did it again, knew exactly what she thought, what she wanted.

"Thanks."

"I want your undivided attention tonight. I want to make it special."

He didn't need to say it but they both knew why he wanted the night to end so perfectly. It would be the last time. The knowledge didn't sit right. Her heart filled with a dread. She felt like her body might explode with the pain.

Luciano walked around the car, grabbed her hand, his grasp somehow eased the pressure inside her body.

They made a quick run through of the store. Everything was perfect, just like it would if Kaylee closed herself. Maria was such an asset to her, an asset she wouldn't have if it wasn't for the man on her arm.

"Look good?" he asked.

"Perfect."

Luciano picked her up taking long, smooth strides to the door. He grabbed the keys from her hand and locked the door with her still tightly in his arms. He ran up the stairs taking them two at a time.

"I'm too heavy for you to do this."

"No way. You feel just right in my arms."

Kaylee giggled as he unlocked her door. Once they crossed the threshold, Luciano had her mouth in a hot, demanding kiss. Kaylee snaked her arms around his neck and through his silken, black hair.

He walked like a man on a mission. He lowered her to the bed, her head sinking into her white, cloud-like pillows.

Luciano followed. He lay on his side next to her, rolling Kaylee over so they faced each other.

"So velvety soft," he whispered against her mouth as his fingers brushed her arm. "I've never touched a woman who is as soft as you. So inviting. I want to drown in you."

"Oh God." She could get used to this, get used to Luciano. She felt so right lying in his arms. *Please don't let this night end.* She kissed him fiercely.

"Slow down, Bella." Luciano pulled away. "I'm savoring you tonight. Kissing you from head to toe."

Her head spun. Her heart raced.

"Just let me kiss you for now." Luciano moved his lips to her jaw, her neck, her ear. "I want to remember every spot you like to be touched. How your body tastes."

Nothing ever sounded so good. "Yes, Luciano. Please."

Kaylee lay still, waiting. He rolled her on her back. Luciano straddled her hips as he slowly raised her shirt over her stomach, his thumb trailing up her belly. "I have to get you naked if I'm going to have free reign on your body. If I want my lips on every inch of you."

His words caressed her body. They touched her as expertly as his hands and lips did. After pulling her shirt over her head, Luciano unclasped the front clasp on her yellow bra, easing it down her arms as well.

Oh God. Luciano moved down her body, his strong hands spreading her legs so he could rest between them. Then his lips were back on hers again, the kiss soft, his tongue gently probing her lips. When her mouth opened, she was treated to his intoxicating taste. He caressed her breast, her bare skin, as if he was trying to memorize her body.

His lips trailed down her neck, Kaylee moaned. She wrapped her arms wrapped around his back while he saturated her body with his touch. Luciano's lips traveled down her body, slowly making his way down her stomach.

When his hands moved to the buttons on her shorts, Kaylee writhed beneath him, the heat shooting through her body was almost unbearable. As if opening a delicate package he popped the button before easing her zipper down. As her shorts eased down her legs, Kaylee watched in anticipation for what Luciano would do next.

Luciano's fingers trembled as he pulled Kaylee's shorts and panties down. The wild thump of his heart could rival a stampede. How would he live without touching her again? How could he never again see her beautiful, bare, brown skin? *It has to be this way.*

"Lovely," he said. "I feel like it's the first time I've seen you." Luciano held her foot while he spoke then dropped his mouth to her ankle. His mouth moved slowly up her leg. On edge, his body burned with desire. He found his utopia with Kaylee writhing beneath him.

"So sweet, Bella." He kissed her again. "Every inch of you is addictive. Like the best chocolate." He kissed behind her knee, easing his lips up her thigh. "I want to devour you."

His lips were almost there, almost to the place he'd wanted to taste for months.

"Yes," Kaylee said breathlessly. "Hurry."

"Not tonight." Luciano held himself in check. His body begged to be inside her. Not yet. Tonight he'd make it last. This time would need to hold him over forever.

Luciano feasted off her thighs and legs, tasting each one evenly before he finally place his mouth at the apex of her thighs. Parting her velvety soft legs as far as he could, Luciano placed a soft kiss above her dark curls before his tongue made its first passionate lick.

Kaylee called out his name.

Luciano struggled to hold his overwhelming desire for her at bay. The sweet sounds she made drove him crazy. Everything about her drove him crazy.

"So sweet." He muttered the words against her heat. When her hands dug into his hair, she loosened the slight grip he had reining his control. Luciano lapped at her, his tongue roaming, seeking all her secrets.

"You feel so good, Luciano." He almost didn't register her words. Her body consumed him so completely.

"It's not me, Bella. It's you. You taste so good."

He swirled his tongue around, exploring all of her, bringing her closer and closer to release. He felt her stiffen against his mouth before screaming his name. It was the most beautiful sound he'd ever heard.

"Wow that was amazing." Kaylee's eyes began to drift closed. Her orgasm almost wiped her out. Her body lay still, deliciously drained, incapable of moving.

"We aren't done yet," Luciano said his mouth finally at her breast. With one lick of his tongue, Kaylee felt her body begin to awaken. Her senses amplified. She felt every lick at her sensitive nipple on every inch of her body. Had it ever felt like this before? No. She knew that as clearly as day. Nothing had ever felt this good and probably never would again. Not with another man.

"I love these pert, little, brown nipples, Kaylee." His sexy, bedroom talk turned her heat up higher.

"I'm glad. They like you too," Kaylee said with a soft laugh.

"I'm glad to hear it."

Kaylee lay there, reveling in Luciano lips on her breasts. First the right then the left and back again. Her body pulsed with pleasure.

"I want to touch you too. I want to feel your skin under my hands." She finally managed to say to him, impatiently pulling her hands under his polo shirt.

"Not yet," he whispered against her breast. "If I take off my clothes, I won't be able to hold myself back."

"Don't hold back," Kaylee said trying to catch him by surprise and rolling over so he lay beneath her.

"You do know I let you do that, don't you? Better access." Luciano lifted his head off the pillow sucking one breast into his mouth. Kaylee teasingly tried to pull away. Luciano's strong hold kept her from moving.

"Going somewhere?" he asked.

Not on your life.

"I didn't think so." He knew her so well. She didn't have to speak a word for him to know her thoughts.

Luciano kissed her nipple again. "What do you do to me?"

Luciano looked serious. "I don't know but you do it to me too."

He pulled her to her feet and Kaylee quickly attacked his shorts. She willed her fingers to ease their shakiness pulling his button free before pulling his zipper down.

"I can't wait anymore," were the only words she could say.

Grabbing his belt loops, Kaylee pulled Luciano's shorts down his legs making sure to take his boxer briefs at the same time. He too looked impatient…eager…ready… He ripped his shirt over his head before throwing it to the floor. Kaylee looked up at him, standing gloriously naked in front of her, her heart telling her what she wanted to deny.

"Sh," Luciano said laying her on the bed before kissing her so sweetly she wanted to melt. "I know."

Did he? She wondered. She had a hard time knowing herself. But she knew he did. This man that she met, liked and wanted to have a fun, care-free relationship with somehow knew her better than anyone else, knew her better than she did herself. At that moment, she felt too good, too right to let the knowledge scare her. Her pleasure increased as Luciano slipped his hand down to the center of her thighs, one finger entering her slowly.

"Just right. So soft and wet," he said against her lips. "I want you so much, Bella." Taking his hand away, Luciano grabbed a condom from her nightstand. When he'd put it there she didn't know, but thank God he didn't have to leave her to grab one.

After ripping the package open with his teeth, he eased it down his engorged shaft before slowly, sensually sinking into her. He just lay there on top of her not moving, his eyes penetrating hers as wholly as his body did. She felt more naked than she ever had. He could no doubt see into her soul and for the first time, she didn't mind, didn't want to hide. That should have scared her.

When he finally began to pump in and out of her the world shifted. Humming echoed through her ears, her body sensitive to every movement. Toes curling, her heart expanded overflowing in her chest. He filled her body perfectly, the pleasure almost too much to handle. She felt him everywhere, body, mind and in her heart.

When she started crying, Luciano kissed the tears away, never altering his slowly, seductive thrusts. God she wished it would last. The tightening in her body began. Slowly, powerfully she spiraled into the most intense climax of her life.

As long as she lived, she would never forget this moment.

Luciano wanted Kaylee to sleep naked in his arms. His body itched to move but determination kept him still. Breath hardly escaped his lips. Kaylee wanted nothing to do with sleeping in the same bed with a man. She made that painfully obvious the last time he laid in her bed. So he lay there, perfectly still, watching her, taking her all in before he had to leave.

Which would be very soon.

Feeling brave or maybe just being stupid, Luciano reached out to stroke her hair, twisting the braids between his fingertips. Why did this night have to end? He loved her. For the first time in his life he'd let himself fall in love with a woman. The perfect woman. Her humor brought joy to his life. Her smiles equally as sweet as her kisses. She was strong, beautiful, smart and hardworking.

If she stayed with him he'd ruin it. Ruin her. He couldn't risk snuffing out such a bright light like the one that shown inside her.

She had a bright, luminescent light in her. He'd seen it tonight. Seen the happiness she had inside her. His dad all but extinguished that joy from his mom's eyes. Even from the pictures of them as a young couple, he could tell how bright her happiness shined. He saw flickers of that light every once in a while, but never the blinding, all-consuming shine she had before his dad hurt her. He couldn't handle the thought of taking the light away from Kaylee.

He just hoped she'd one day embrace it. That she wouldn't be afraid to let herself live. He hoped she would find a man worthy of her.

His heart heavy, Luciano placed light feathery kisses across her face; on her forehead, nose, cheeks, and finally her lips. Slowly he rose from the bed and picked up his clothes. When he reached for the door, Luciano turned one last time to look at her laying in the bed. When he saw her again, things would be different. Distant. Lonely. His already weakened defenses crumbled more with the thought.

"Goodbye, Bella," he said before walking out of the room. He quickly and quietly dressed in the bathroom and slipped from her apartment forever.

Chapter Thirteen

"**D**amn it." Kaylee woke up angry, rolling over to realize Luciano wasn't there. For the first time in her life she'd spent the night with a man. For the first time she wished he was still there in the morning. Her anger soon disappeared replaced with a deep sadness. Their relationship was over. It became too dangerous.

Burrowing under the blanket Kaylee fought tears as the scent of Luciano surrounded her, masculine and sweet. She'd never cried over a man before, never given that much control over to someone else.

When Luciano kissed her tears away it almost made them worth it. It actually felt good to have him care about her, to take care of her. Now it was gone. *What am I thinking*? How many times did her mom think she found someone who really cared about her, who would never hurt her? In the end she always played the fool. She always came away with pain rather than the love she so craved.

It's better this way, she told herself. They'd end it now before it had gone further than a casual affair. *Luciano would never hurt you*. A voice that sounded like her own spoke in her head. She wanted to believe that, in some ways she did believe it, but fear overrode her hope. She hated the fear, didn't want to be scared of anything. Fear made her feel weak. Weakness made her feel like her mom.

Stop thinking about this! You have a life to get back to. Rolling out of bed, Kaylee took a quick shower and dressed for the day determined to get to work and put Luciano out of her mind. When she opened the door to head down to the store her mother stood on the other side, hand raised to knock.

Oh God. "What are you doing here, Mom?"

Kaylee watched as Anne Daniels walked into her apartment before taking a seat on the couch. To Kaylee's surprise, she looked good, strong, her head held a bit higher than usual. She wore a pair of black slacks and a silky white blouse. Her hair styled straight, cut in a short bob at her shoulders.

They lived in the same town but rarely made time to see each other.

If Kaylee calculated right, it had been about ten months since they'd last talked.

"Did I teach you to talk to me like that, child?" Anne said crossing her legs.

Is it just me or does she look nervous? Kaylee sat down on the chair beside her.

"Sorry Mama. I had a long night. I'm really shocked to see you."

"How's that store of yours going, anyway?"

Like you care. "Great. Business is booming. I couldn't be happier."

"Good…good. I'm happy to hear that." Her words sounded sincere. "What about dating? You have a man in your life?"

Wow, Anne Daniels just set a record. It took her exactly three minutes to get to the subject of men. "I well…No. There isn't anyone. I'm too busy for a man, Mama."

"You're never too busy for a good man, Kaylee. When's the last time you've dated anyone? You need something in your life besides that store of yours."

Calm yourself. Take a couple of deep breaths so you don't say anything you will regret. "Maybe you don't know all there is to know about me. I actually was dating someone for awhile."

A smile formed on Anne Daniels's face. "Good for you. You need that."

Kaylee rolled her eyes. Would she ever change? Would Anne Daniels ever realize it took more than a man to make you truly happy? She doubted it. Her mom didn't know her at all. "My happiness doesn't depend on a man like yours does."

Her mom flinched.

For the first time since Kaylee could remember she saw a hint of remorse in her mom eyes. She let herself soften. Despite all the pain her mom had caused her Kaylee didn't want to be spiteful.

"I'm sorry. You're right. You never were anything like me. You've always thought you were better than me." Anne stood and walked over to the bookshelf. She studied the books.

"I have a lot of regrets in my life, Kaylee. More than I can count. But I always loved you. I just didn't love myself."

Remorse coursed through Kaylee's body. It hurt to say nasty things to her mom whether she believed them or not. "I'm sorry, Mama. I shouldn't have said that."

"No. You should have said it a long time ago."

Kaylee watched as her mom wiped a tear away.

"I know you probably don't believe me, but I've gone through a lot of changes this past year."

Oh God, it was a year since she'd last seen her own mother. The cruelty overwhelmed her.

"I hit rock bottom right after the last time we saw each other. I lost my job, lost my apartment, lost my mind for a while there."

Her mom had lost her apartment and Kaylee didn't know? "Why didn't you tell me?" Kaylee asked.

"Like I said, I hit rock bottom but it took hitting that bottom for me to learn to swim towards the surface. I finally got tired of depending on other people. I knew I had to start depending on myself. I started seeing a counselor a couple times a week trying to find out why I did the things I did. I won't give you all the details but I found out a lot about myself. Realized how much I hurt you. I needed to change, Sweet Pea.

Tears started to flow from Kaylee's eyes. When was the last time her mom called her sweet pea? Ten, twelve years ago?

"Anyway, I started concentrating on myself. Started to be strong by myself. I've made a great deal of progress. I did the counseling two times a week for four months. Now I only go once every other week. It helped a lot."

"Why didn't you tell me?"

"Scared probably. I wanted to be sure I had my head on straight, for good this time. I got a job at a little flower shop. I love it. The woman who owns it has taught me everything there is to know about flowers, making arrangements, that kind of thing." Her mom finally turned to face her.

"It's the first time I've been interested in something since I was young. I can make anything beautiful with flowers."

"How long have you been there?" Kaylee asked.

"Eight months."

"That's great, Mama. I'm happy," Kaylee said meaning it. How many times had she wished to see her mom standing on her own? Too many to count.

"I'm sorry for all the times I hurt you, Sweet Pea. I'm sorry about the men, about the depression, about all of it. You didn't deserve that and I hope I can make it up to you now."

Heart pounding, her tears began to race down her face. Happy tears. She hadn't realized how much she missed her mom, how much she wanted her mom in her life.

"Its okay, Mama. I'm just so happy you're here now."

Her mom wrapped her arms around her. Kaylee felt safe, loved, like just maybe there was more to life than her bookstore. Hugging her mom back with all her might, they stood there rocking and crying.

"This is a happy time," Anne Daniels said to her daughter. She grabbed her hand and brought her to the chair so she could sit. She

took the seat across on the sofa once again. "I'm thinking about opening my own flower shop if I can get the money. I really think I've
found something I'm good at."

The words filled Kaylee with joy. Her mom found something she
liked other than men. It felt good and gave Kaylee a hope that maybe
she could let herself find, or accept the one thing she found that made
her happy besides her bookstore. "I'm so happy for you, Mama. I'd
love to see some of your work some time."

A bright light flashed in her mom's eyes and a full-fledged smile
curved her lips. "I'd like that, sweet pea. More than you know."
Changing the subject, Anne said, "So tell me about this man you're
dating."

"Its nothing," Kaylee said drying her eyes. "Just a little fling.
Actually, it's over now."

"The look in your eyes tells me it's more than a fling."

Oh God, she wished. "No, Mama. Really, it was just a fling."

"Well, I have some more news for you," her mom said.

Dread coursed through Kaylee's body at her words. She had a feeling she wasn't going to like this. How sad, just seconds ago she felt so
undeniably happy. Felt like she and her mom had a future together,
could maybe even become close.

"What is it?"

"Before I tell you, I just want you to know it's different this time.
This isn't like all the other times."

No, no, no! This isn't fair!

"The woman who owns the flower shop I work at? She has a son
my age. We've been dating for about five months now. We really got
to know each other. He spent time at the store with me, he urges me to
continue what I'm doing, he knows about my past. He's a really special man, Sweet Pea and well, he's asked me to marry him, and I said
yes."

Kaylee took a couple of shallow, near hyperventilating breaths. The
tears that had dried now flowed again but now they were tears of sadness.

"How many times have I heard that before? He's special? Please
Mom. How stupid do you think I am?" Then to herself she said, "God,
I can't believe I almost fell for this." Kaylee buried her face in her
hands unable to look at her mom.

"There's nothing to fall for. It's the truth. I found myself before I
found Michael. I know I could live without him, but I don't want to.
It's not like before. I don't think the sun rises and sets on him. We actually have things in common. He encourages my self development, my
counseling. If you'd just take the time to meet him, you'd see the dif-

ference. Don't close me out, Kaylee. I want so much for you to be happy for me."

"Happy for you?" Kaylee stood pacing again. "How can I be happy when I know I'll be picking up the pieces when this all falls apart? I'll be the one wiping your tears when you think the world's over because this man left you." Her words were harsh, but true. She always had to pick up the pieces for her mom. She was always more the parent than the child.

"I wish you could have a little bit of faith in me, Sweet Pea. I'm truly happy for the first time in my life and I'd like nothing more than to share it with you."

I want to believe you, but I'm scared. Scared I'll get hurt again.

"I can't be a part of this, Mama. I can't do it. I think its time for you to go. My store opens soon and I need to get down there." Her words sounded as detached as she wished she felt.

Anne set a piece of paper on the table. "Here's my phone number at home and at the store in case you ever want to use it. I'm leaving an invitation here for you as well. If you change your mind, the wedding is in three weeks." With sad eyes, she walked out of the apartment.

Kaylee, Bri, and Tabby sat in her living room. She hadn't thought she'd have to tell them this soon but since they showed up she figured she better get it over with. "We can't go to Luciano's anymore," Tabby and Brianna looked at Kaylee open-mouthed because of her words.

"Why's that?" Brianna asked.

"It's over between us. I think it will be too awkward to keep going there." Awkward and hard but she didn't tell them that part. They wouldn't understand, no one did.

"I thought you guys had this whole thing worked out, Kay? Wasn't it supposed to be this easy affair that wouldn't change anything? Now we all have to switch our routine around," Tabby said with frustration.

Annoyance gripped Kaylee. "I'm sorry to ruin your weekly Nico drool fest, Tab. Let me rephrase my sentence, I can't go to Luciano's anymore. You two can still go on Friday's if it's that important." *Why am I taking my anger out on them? They're all I have left.*

"Relax, girl. You're trippin' out on the wrong people here," Bri tried to calm her. "What's going on all of a sudden? You two were getting pretty hot and heavy."

I finally woke up. I finally remembered that relationships aren't for me. I'm so scared I'm going to be like my mom. "Nothing's going on. We all knew Luciano and I wouldn't last long. End of story."

"Well, I didn't know we wouldn't be able to continue our Friday night ritual when it was over. I told you this was a bad idea from the beginning. Sex isn't something to take lightly."

"Tabby, I'm really not in the mood for a lecture on true love and following you're heart. This isn't an after school special."

Bri held up her hand. "Okay, that's enough you two. Who'd have ever thought I'd be the one playing the peacekeeper."

Kaylee plopped down on her couch, thankful her friends showed up even though she had a hard time showing it. Somehow they knew she needed them but all she wanted to do was push them away. *This is Bri and Tab. They're always here. Don't push them away.*

"I'm sorry," Kaylee sniffled. "I had the worst day." The girls sat on either side of her. "Luciano and I already decided we wouldn't see each other again. It's just not something either of us can risk." Turning to look at Tabby she continued, "God I wanted to try though. I wanted us to be able to keep things going the way they were."

"What happened?" Bri put her hand around her shoulder.

"My mom." Tabby and Bri cursed but Kaylee continued. "I was so stupid. She came to me, told me how she's changed, that for the first time she could stand on her own two feet, that she had a job she really enjoyed. I wanted so much to believe her."

"Of course you did. She's still your mom no matter what, Kay," Tabby told her.

"I know. I did believe her at first. Then she dropped the bomb. She's getting married...again! This is number five and that doesn't even count the numerous relationships between. I can't risk it...I can't risk being like her."

Tears rolled down her face. After the day spent crying she thought they'd run dry, but they still flowed freely. Bri and Tabby sat there quiet, Tabby with her hand on her knee and Bri had one on her shoulder.

"She told me she's been going to counseling, that she realized how much she hurt me, hurt herself, that she didn't feel like she needed a man to be strong anymore. How can that be if she's getting married again? No one, not even me, has ever meant more to her than a man." Kaylee lowered her face in her hands.

"Maybe things are different this time, Kay. Maybe she's healed so she can actually be a part of a real, healthy relationship with a man."

Tabby's words were spoken softly as if she was afraid Kaylee would go off on her. Right now she didn't have the strength.

"Things will never change. "Kaylee said. "Not for her and not for me. It's time we both face that."

Luciano sat at his desk trying with no luck to finish his paperwork. The week passed by in a blur. Friday had come and gone and Kaylee didn't make an appearance. All night he checked the door, held their table, wished she'd show and then condemned himself for that wish, and still she never came. *It's probably easier this way.* He knew it would be easier this way, but damn it still hurt. He didn't mean to, but he'd fallen, hard.

Nico rode him hard all week about his moping around. He didn't feel the same and wondered if he ever would again. Had he been happy before meeting Kaylee? He thought he was but now he wasn't sure. Things looked different now; he missed her touch, her smile, her laugh. He missed it all but was too afraid to do anything about it. *You'll hurt her. You'll neglect her. Hell, you might even up and leave her one day.* He didn't want that. She deserved better.

"Hey man," Nico said letting himself into the office. Luciano's had been closed an hour. They were alone in the restaurant. "Why don't you just call her?"

Luciano let himself speak freely. "Why don't you layoff? We aren't having this conversation again."

"You aren't happy, Lu. Admit it. While you and Kaylee were together you were happy for the first time in years."

Nico was right, he hadn't been happy before. Nico noticed it. A heavy weight lay on his chest. "I'll hurt her, Nic. I have no idea how to be in a real relationship with a woman. You've heard it as much as I have. I'm just like my dad."

"Not about that you aren't. You look like him; you share his name, some of his personality traits, but not all of them."

Luciano rubbed his face. "I can't risk her heart because you don't think I'm like him. I know I am. I feel it."

Nico exhaled a breath and cursed. "It was different without them tonight. I know you felt it."

"I'm not denying it." Luciano ran a hand through his hair before leaning back in the chair. "See if one of the other chefs can pick up some more hours. I think I need a little vacation. Do you think you can hold down the fort for me?" He needed to get out of there for a while.

"Sure, buddy. Whatever you want."

Nico traipsed the restaurant engaging customers, his eyes darting to the door every time the bell rang wondering when Tabby would show. Luciano had left a week ago and he hadn't heard a word from him since. Worried about his cousin, Nico called Tabby wondering if Kaylee had heard from him. He kept himself from calling Kaylee himself not wanting to scare her. If he knew women as well as he thought he did, Kaylee loved Luciano as much as Luciano loved her.

The bell jingled, somehow sounding livelier than the other jingles, so he knew it was Tabby. Meeting her at the door he informed the hostess he planned to take a quick break before she walked off to seat a customer.

"Thanks for coming," he said to Tabby taking in her tight black dress, her long hair tied back in some kind of twist thing on the back of her head. Hot. He became instantly hard.

"Sure, although I'm kind of curious why you needed to talk to me."

"Let's head back to Luciano's office. I don't want to talk out in the open." Nico put his hand at the small of her back, right above her curved backside to lead her into the office. Unfortunately, but not to his surprise, she pulled away from him. "You act like I bite, sweetheart. I promise, I won't, unless you ask that is," he said with a wink.

"If that's why you asked me to come, I'll just turn around and leave now. I don't play musical dates like you do."

Did she sound disappointed? Something about her voice suggested she was. *Probably just wishful thinking.*

"This way," Nico told her as they turned into Luciano's office and he closed the door behind them. "Listen, Luciano took off a week ago and I haven't heard from him. I'm wondering if Kaylee mentioned anything to you. Maybe she's heard from him or something?"

Tabby shook her head. "No. I know she hasn't talked to him since the music festival. God, I hope he's okay."

"Don't worry too much," he tried to reassure her. "I'm sure he's fine. Just broken-hearted, won't admit it, and doesn't know what to do about it." Then more to himself he added, "And people wonder why I avoid relationships."

"Maybe you should try avoiding sex, too. Seems like that's what got Kay and Luciano in this mess to begin with."

Nico stood there baffled. She could be really outspoken when she wanted to be. Leaning towards her he said, "I didn't know you had so much interest in my sex life, sweetheart. If you'd like to experience it first hand, that can be arranged."

She swatted his arm. "Men! You're all scrubs, aren't you?"

At that moment he had an overwhelming urge to kiss her. *This is not the time for that.*

Nico backed away from temptation in a black dress. "I didn't call you here for all of this. I'm just worried about my cousin. Wishing things could be different for him."

"I know," Tabby said her sincerity obvious. "I wish the same thing for Kaylee. She has so many demons she needs to face."

"Looks like we have something in common then. The question is what can we do about it?"

Her eyes brightened. He knew she was one of those mushy, romantic women. "We need to try and get them together. I know Kaylee loves him. She's just too afraid to give herself over to someone so completely."

"When you put it like that, it sounds damn scary to me too. Maybe I should rethink this," he said with a smile.

"Agh. You're so bad, Nico."

"It feels good to be bad, sweetheart. You should give it a try."

"Do you ever stop flirting?"

He laughed. "Not when I'm around you."

Tabby held up her hand. "That's enough. We need to concentrate on Kaylee and Luciano. I want to see her happy. No one deserves it more than she does."

"So does Luciano."

"What's the plan?"

"You work on Kaylee. Try to soften her up. And try to get her back in this restaurant. Once I find Luciano, I'll see what I can do on my end," he shook his head. "I know it's not much of a plan, but it's a start."

Tabby smiled at him and he hardened even more. She looked so sweet, so sincere, so hot. "Thanks for calling me. It means a lot that you care about Luciano and Kaylee this much."

He took a step forward to kiss her gently. Her soft lips felt tense then seconds later they softened until she began to kiss him back. He palmed her head to deepen the kiss right when the door flew open. Tabby pulled away just in time to keep whoever walked in from knowing what they were doing.

"Nico," came a high-pitched, valley-girl voice that he recognized immediately. "I was really upset you had to break our date, but oh so glad when you invited me here instead."

Shit. Cindy. How did he forget he invited her here tonight?

"Um, hey Cindy. I'm doing some business. Can I have a minute and I'll be out?" he asked.

"Sure thing, cutie. Just give me one kiss to hold me over." Before Nico could stop her, Cindy grabbed his shirt and laid one on him. Nico jerked away trying not to hurt the girl's feelings and hoping like hell he didn't hurt Tabby.

"I'll see myself out," Tabby said before she smacked him across the face and walked out the door.

Luciano turned up the air conditioning in his car hoping to wake himself up. The never ending stretches of Southern California highways started to all blur together. He'd been driving around for days, thinking, missing Kaylee and feeling sorry for himself.

It had been a long time since he'd let himself feel like this. It didn't feel good.

Nothing had changed and he knew it never would. But still, he needed to go home. He needed to move on with his life, get back involved with what was the most important thing in his life, Luciano's. Pulling his black Mercedes around sharply he headed back towards San Francisco.

He'd go home for a day, spend some time with his mom, and then get on with his life. The drive to his mom's house didn't take as long as he'd imagined. Pulling up to the curb he took in the familiar site of home. Getting out and walking inside he realized how much he needed to see him mom.

"Oh, Luciano. Where have you been? I've been calling you for days," Isabelle Valenti said as Luciano walked in the door. She kissed his cheeks before rushing him into the kitchen. "What do you want to eat?"

"I smell the sauce cooking. I'll just take that with some macaroni." He knew better than to turn down food from his mom even if he wasn't particularly hungry. "I took a ride for a few days, Mama. I needed a little break. That's all."

Luciano watched his mama move around the small kitchen scooping macaroni on his plate. Her kitchen smelled better than *Luciano's* did. A mixture of sweet spices always permeated the air when he came home. Lately he hadn't made it home as much as he liked. Isabelle was a small woman, physically. Standing about five foot one inch but with more personality than he carried in his little finger.

He watched as his mother walked toward him and place the plate in front of him. After taking a seat herself, she took one look at him and asked, "Who is she?"

"This is good sauce," Luciano replied while taking a bite.

"Of course its good sauce. Now quit changing the subject and don't talk with your mouth full."

Damn. Why'd I come here? He knew she'd know. Maybe deep down he wanted her to know, wanted to talk to her about it.

"You gave me food and asked me a question. How am I not supposed to talk with my mouth full?"

"Fine, the food can wait," she replied pulling the plate away.

"It's nothing. Nothing you need to worry yourself with anyway."

Isabelle reached out to grab her son's hand, her small, delicate fingers barely reaching around his wrist.

"Anything that concerns you, concerns me. Especially if it brings that emptiness back into your eyes."

A slideshow of thoughts played through Luciano's mind. "Her name's Kaylee. She's a woman I was dating for awhile. It didn't work out." He tried to simplify the situation.

"You mean you didn't let it work out. Are you so afraid of happiness?"

Damn the woman for being so blunt. His head shook from side to side. "I'm not afraid of being happy. I'm afraid of who I am, afraid of hurting her. She's special." Luciano squeezed his mom's hand. "You'd like her."

Water pooled in her eyes. "I really messed things up for you didn't I?"

How can she blame herself? "You didn't do anything wrong. My father did. He forgot about you, he pushed you aside, taking advantage of all you did for him. Then he abandoned you." Anger laced his words.

"But I took it. I let you live with it, see it, fearing you'd become it."

"I am my father's son," he spit the words out.

"You share my blood too. You have a gentle heart, Luciano. You would never hurt your Kaylee."

"How can I be sure?" God he wanted to believe her.

"You know in here." Isabelle let loose of his hand to touch his chest. "You know just as well as I know it."

"It's not as easy as that, Mama."

"Why not? Because you decided it had to be hard? It doesn't. What have you done to your Kaylee that makes you think you'd hurt her?"

Luciano watched his mom, thinking about what she said. "Nothing. I haven't given myself the chance yet."

"In the time you've dated this young woman there's never been a chance where you could be there for her but you chose to forget her for yourself? Have you abandoned her when she needed you?"

"No." *Where is she going with this?*

"What about that earthquake? I called the restaurant that day. Imagine my surprise when Nicky told me you were with a woman, helping her rather than being at Luciano's?"

Damn Nico. Now he knew why his Mama knew he had a woman in his life. Not that he was surprised Nico told her. Their families were so close. Not that Nico could keep a secret anyway.

"Big deal. I knew the restaurant was fine." *You can't change my mind on this, Mama.*

"Do you think that would stop some people? You stayed for her because you care about her. You put her happiness above your own.

Give yourself credit for that."

"You should have seen how upset she was. You would have done the same thing."

"Yes, I would have. Would your father?"

He'd walked right into that one. She did have a point, but how could he risk her future on one little circumstance? He couldn't. Not when he knew what he was.

"You've always had a big heart. You took care of me, you've been there for Nicky, I know you'd be there for your Kaylee too."

"Thanks, Mama." Luciano lowered his head. "I'm scared. I really think I love her and I don't think I could live with myself if I hurt her." He couldn't remember ever sounding or feeling so broken before.

"Listen to your own words, son. You feel so much but you try to hide it. Embrace it; embrace your feelings for this girl. You deserve to be happy."

Two weeks ago he would have said he already had all the happiness in the world. Now, he knew different. While *Luciano's* made him happy, it didn't compare to the joy Kaylee brought. *I want to be happy.*

"You fear hurting her, yet you can't imagine doing it," Isabelle said. "Why do you fear something you don't think you could ever do?"

"Did you think Dad would hurt you the way he did. Do you think he did?"

"You are two separate species. When I dated your father things were different. If you got pregnant, you got married. We did what was expected of us, even though I knew he never loved me. I thought I could love enough for the both of us." New tears began to form in her eyes. "We were young, having fun, and that's the way he wanted things to stay. Our families had something else in mind. Your father did what was expected of him then closed himself off to me, to us."

Disgust ate him from the inside out. "What kind of man would do that?" he asked.

"Not you. Don't pass up love because you're scared of something you could never become. I wasted my whole live in love with a man who never loved me. I suffered and my son suffered because of it. If you never found happiness I'd blame myself for the rest of my life."

The last person in the world he wanted to hurt was his mom. She'd been everything to him his whole life. He wanted to be the person she believed him to be. He wanted his mom to be proud of him as much as he wanted to make Kaylee happy.

I love her.

God! How could he have been so stupid? How could he fear being the same as a man he detested? Mama believed in him. Nico, Maria, everyone he knew believed in him and counted on him. Had he ever let them down? If everyone else could believe in him couldn't he believe in himself?

"Finally starting to see?" Isabelle whispered. "I see it in your eyes."

A thought struck him for the first time. "What if she won't have me? What if she doesn't love me?"

"You'll never know if you don't talk to her. Is she worth the risk?"

More than she knew. She'd make him the man he wanted to be. "She's worth everything." Luciano jumped to his feet, bent to kiss his mom on the cheek before striding for the door. "Thanks, Mama.

Chapter Fourteen

"**G**irl, I think you've finally lost it. You're officially crazy," Kaylee said into the cordless phone at Bookends. Somehow, Anne and Tabby were in contact. Somehow, she managed to get to her friend. *Not gonna work, Mom. Talking to Tabby and Bri won't get me to go to your wedding.*

"I think it would be healing for you," Tabby told her. "I think your mom has really changed this time and maybe if you see her happiness you'll go after your own."

"Who needs Oprah when I have you, Tab? Maybe you should think about starting your own talk show."

"You know, you're starting to sound more and more like Brianna lately. I'm trying to be a friend here."

Damn. "You're right, Tab. I'm sorry. I just don't need to hear this. You're asking too much." Tabby didn't understand. She had the perfect childhood with perfect, loving parents. She couldn't understand what it was like for Kaylee as a child.

"Think about it, would ya? What can it hurt to go to the wedding? No matter what, she's still your mom."

Believe me, I know. "I'll think about it, Tab."

"That's all I'm asking. The wedding and the reception."

Tricky, Tricky. "You're doing me wrong here, girl. Started out with the wedding, now it's the wedding and the reception." Could she do it? Was she really promising to think about going to her mom's fifth wedding? God, five weddings! The thought made her skin crawl.

"The reception should go without saying. If you're going to the wedding of course you'll go to the reception."

"Where's it at?" Kaylee asked.

Tabby didn't answer for a good ten seconds. As the silence stretched out, Kaylee felt the hairs on the back of her neck stand. Something didn't seem right. "Tabby?"

"We're still working on that."

The bell over *Bookends* door jingled. As Kaylee turned around to greet her customer her heart leapt into her throat. Her body betraying her began to tingle with delight.

Luciano.

"I have to go, Tab," Kaylee said hanging up the phone without waiting for a response.

Luciano sauntered into the store looking sinfully fine in a pair of black pants and a white shirt. His hair loose around his face just the way she liked it.

"What the hell are you doing?" Kaylee asked as she watched him turn her open sign to closed.

"Hand me the keys."

"No. I'm not closing my store. I have work to do." Oh God it felt good to see him. Her body felt light, she sizzled. Her stomach fluttered with butterflies, her skin heated remembering his touch.

Luciano walked behind the counter like he owned the place. His long legs making the trek in a few steps. As he walked past she inhaled a deep breath of sexy, strong, Italian man.

Kaylee stood still as a statue as he grabbed the keys from under the register and walked over to the door to lock it. *Lord, give me strength, because I'm going to need it.*

"We need to talk."

"I don't know what we'd have to talk about." Kaylee attempted to sound casual, stacking books on the counter. Really she felt anything but casual. Her body was edgy, wanting.

"Damn, I didn't think it would be this weird between us," Luciano sat on the couch. "I should have known though. After how intense that last night was, I should have known you'd hide from me."

Whipping around to face him, Kaylee lost the ability to speak. The anger, the frustration, the pain, all disappeared and was replaced by a foreign emotion. One she didn't want to name.

Snapping herself back into reality she said, "I don't hide from anyone." If only that were true.

"Wrong, Bella. Sit down; I have a few things I need to tell you."

"Really, Luciano, I—"

"Please?"

The pain in his voice almost ripped her apart. Her heart ached for him, for whatever brought the strained look in his eyes, for her because she could never have this man she truly wanted.

Kaylee sat down on the couch next to Luciano. Her body already reacted to his scent swirling around her, his warmth caressing her arms, if she looked at him, she just might do something stupid.

Why did he affect her so intensely? Her body was on a hair trigger whenever he neared her. She wanted so badly to reach over and touch him, kiss him, make love to him.

"I've missed you, Bella."

How could his voice still sound so calm, so smooth? She felt close to leaping out of her own skin.

"You didn't miss me, Luciano. It's not like we were dating..." Then why did she miss him too?

"Why won't you look at me?"

Luciano's warm hand reached out and cupped her cheek. Kaylee leaned her cheek against his hand and the pad of his thumb began to draw circles on her cheek.

"Look at me," he whispered.

Kaylee soaked in the feel of Luciano's hand caressing her skin, trying to take it all in. His voice calling out to her she turned to face him. *Don't do it. Don't look him in the eyes*. Too late, the deep, dark chocolate already pulled her in, she drowned in their depths.

"What...what did you come here for Luciano?" she asked.

She listened as he took a deep breath, felt the cool, minty air as he exhaled hard. "I'm not willing to let you go, Bella. Not without a fight."

His words shocked her from her passion induced state. Leaping out of his reach, Kaylee backed up on the couch. She stared in astonishment at Luciano as a smile stretched across his face. What did he mean? What about what he'd told her about his dad? Why did he smile? *Maybe he's playing a joke on me*.

"Sweet, Bella, I missed you."

His smile grew as he grabbed her hands. Right now, she couldn't control her body so she didn't have any choice but to allow him to lead her.

Still unable to speak, Kaylee sat there staring at Luciano.

"You have no idea how much I wanted to stay with you that last night. How much I wanted to hold you. How much I wished I didn't have to walk away." Luciano still held her hand. "I've been such a fool. But I refuse to be a fool any longer. We're good together, Bella. You know it as well as I do. I'm not willing to throw that away just because I'm scared."

Kaylee found her voice. "What about your dad? What about what you told me?"

"I'm not him. I could never be. I don't know why I didn't see it before. Maybe it took *you* to finally make me realize. Maybe it took love...but I know now. Life's too short to be afraid. God, I want to be happy. I want you to be happy. We can give that to each other, Bella."

Love? She yearned to hold him tight and tell him she loved him. Fear held her back. She didn't want to be scared anymore, but didn't know how to change it.

"I can't, Luciano." Shaking her hand free of his grasp she continued, "Don't you see? I'm not made that way. We'd never work. In the end I'd end up hurt and alone because I depended on someone else. I can't give you that power over me."

For the first time in her life, she wished she could. Wished she wasn't always so untrusting, wished she could depend on someone, let herself need someone. That just wasn't in the cards. Not for her.

"You can, Bella. I don't want power over you, I want to love you."

Oh God. Dizziness overtook her. Kaylee leaned back into the couch. "If you don't let me down, I'll let you down. Maybe that's really the way it's been all along anyway."

"Who hurt you, Bella? Who made you so afraid to trust someone? So afraid to depend on anyone?"

Could she tell him? No one knew about her mom, about all the men, except for Tabby and Bri. They were the only people she'd ever trusted. Could she trust Luciano? *You owe him that, Kay. He opened his heart to you.* "I..." *Open your mouth and talk.*

"I can't be like my mom, so weak, so needy." *Aren't you being weak now*? "She was never happy on her own. The whole time I was growing up she had men in and out of the house. She'd know them a week and they'd move in. She'd get married after a month. Every time she promised it would be different. She promised this was *the one.*

"As a child I remember her telling me all women need a man to take care of them. She kept looking for a man to take care of us instead of trying to do it herself. All the guys she picked where losers. Half didn't have jobs. Hell, half the time she couldn't hold down a job. Some of the men made me call them daddy. I hated that."

This is so hard. As if sensing her pain, Luciano reached out, grabbing her hand, brushing her braids back with his other. "She'd act so happy when she had a new man in her life, she'd smile, dress up, she'd even make me do the same thing. In the beginning I loved it. It was like this high. Like life would finally be right. But then the fighting would start." Kaylee stopped trying to compose herself. *Be a woman. Don't cry.*

"Keep going, Bella," Luciano's voice whispered with emotion.

"They'd fight, the man would leave and I'd be there to pick up the pieces. I'd wipe her tears, I'd tell her everything would be okay. I cooked everyday, I got myself ready for school in the morning, I learned to be responsible for myself. Pretty soon, it started to feel really good. Better than anything I'd ever known. I didn't depend on anyone from age thirteen on. Just myself."

They sat in silence. Kaylee amazed she'd told him, tried to get a hold on herself. She needed to close off the emotions Luciano somehow made her open up. They overwhelmed her, they were just as strong and just as painful as if they'd happened yesterday. *I'm weak just like her. Why can't I get past this*? Thankfully Luciano didn't push her. He let her set the pace.It would be so easy to let herself love him, and she did. She had to keep her emotions in check, pushing all her feelings into a little box to store inside her heart. *Get over it*.

"So now you know my sob story," Kaylee pulled her hand away again and rose off the couch. "I know it sounds crazy, to still carry all that around with me after all those years, but I can't forget it. I refuse to let myself become her."

"You're too strong to be like her, Bella. Can't you see that? If I can get over my past you can too."

"No, I can't. Guess I'm not as strong as you thought." Kaylee began organizing books, putting herself into mannequin mode.

"Don't close yourself off," Luciano pleaded walking towards her, reaching out his arms to try and hold her.

"Don't," Kaylee put her hand up. "I'm happy for you. Happy you found whatever answers you needed and things turned around well for you, but that's not me. I have all the answers I need and that's not going to change. All I need is myself and my bookstore," the harshness in her voice enforced the coat of armor she wore. A knight didn't have anything on her. Kaylee had her full coat of arms and shield intact.

The four walls of the bookstore began to close in around her making Luciano seem unbearably close. His scent invaded her, his warmth rolling off him in waves around her.

"Can you honestly tell me you don't love me?" Luciano asked.

No. "It doesn't matter if I do. Nothing changes."

"Believe me, Bella. It matters."

"Kaylee. Please, call me Kaylee now," she said trying to close herself off as much as possible. "I need you to go, Luciano. I can't do this." He stared at her, his eyes probing deep into her soul. "Please?" *I sound so weak.*

"I love you." Luciano leaned forward, his lips capturing hers for a soul-stirring kiss before he turned and walked out the door. The scariest part, she missed his touch already.

Luciano dug his keys out of his pocket. Pain was etched into Kaylee's features as Luciano turned to walk out the door. She hadn't said she didn't love him. His light at the end of the tunnel. If she didn't care she would have said so. Still, did he go after her or give her space? Right now, she needed space. Space to sort through her feelings, space to come to terms with his.

Climbing into his car Luciano pulled away from the curb to head to the restaurant. Damn, he hadn't made his way there yet since coming home. First he'd driven by the house to shower and change, his second destination, Kaylee.

Now he needed to head over to Luciano's, see how things had held up during his absence and see Nico. Nico had saved his ass plenty in the last couple weeks. More than he'd ever needed to before. Usually Luciano saved Nico. How the roles had reversed. Luciano was the one chasing a woman while Nico concentrated on the restaurant. The only difference, Luciano had ended up falling in love.

Laughing sarcastically Luciano pulled into the restaurant parking lot and headed inside. For the first time in his life he'd fallen in love. He'd not only found the woman he wanted to spend the rest of his life with, but also realized he wasn't the monster whose blood ran through his veins.

"Well look who decided to grace us with his presence," Nico said to him as he rounded the corner into the kitchen.

"Hey, Nic."

"Hey Nic? All I get is a "hey Nic"? Do you know how busy I've been since you've been gone? Not to mention I've been worried sick."

Luciano laughed, the sound not ringing true. "I fell in love. Told the woman I love how I felt only to be turned down, then come to work to have my cousin playing the nagging wife. Just my luck."

"Back up a minute there," Nico said dragging him into a pantry. "Can you repeat that?"

Luciano ran his hand through his hair. "You heard me."

"Where the hell did you go?"

"It doesn't matter. I've realized you were right. Thank you for trying to open my eyes. I'm a better man than my father ever was. I want to prove that, to myself and to Kaylee." He watched the look of shock spread across Nico's face.

"I'm glad, man. A little shocked, but happy."

"Don't be. I haven't won her heart yet."

"You will, boss."

Luciano wasn't so sure. "Enough of that for now. How have things been here?"

"Great. No major problems. I do have a bit of news though."

"What's up?"

"We're hosting a wedding reception here. I'm cooking. They rented out the whole place. I know we've never done that but we have talked about it. I made an executive decision."

Luciano thought for a minute. "Good call, Nic. I'm turning over a new leaf. Might as well turn one over at work too."

"Damn," Kaylee muttered as she dropped a load of books onto her foot. "Get it together, girl." Even though Luciano had sauntered out of her store the week before, he hadn't left her. His smell lingered on the couch pillows making her body pulse with desire. His words echoed through her head, over and over. His warmth, his touch, his eyes, his kiss…everything about him lingered.

Oh God, his kiss. If she kept up on this route, she'd be closing down her store to enter the loony bin. Her body confused with the feelings that stirred there. Kaylee picked up the books, before plopping down on the couch. Why? Why couldn't she be as strong as him? Why couldn't she forget her past? Why couldn't she be as strong as the image she tried so hard to project to the world?

Maybe Tab and Bri are right. No, how could it help to forgive her mom? How would it help to sit down and witness what would no doubt be a pseudo marriage? How hard could it be with her girls by her side?

What about Luciano? He'd found a way to get over his past. Could she do the same thing? Bri and Tab seemed to think she was strong enough. They thought it started with forgiving her mom, with going to the wedding. Luciano thought her strong too. God she'd fooled them all. Especially Luciano. The man who said he loved her.

It took everything she had not to give in and tell him how she felt. In the end her fear won out, gripped her too tightly to break free. *Strangled is more like it.* She hated living like that. Scared and weak. Locking the doors of the store, Kaylee walked up to her apartment thoughts still bombarding her brain. As she walked in the door the rapid blink of the red light on her answering matching caught her attention.

Bri or Tabby would have called her downstairs at the store so who could it be? Pushing the button she listened to a familiar voice. One that made her skin tingle in anticipation.

"Bella? It's Luciano. I'm not giving up. I'd like to see you. Call me?" his words ended with the click of his phone.

"I'm not giving up. I'm not giving up," his smooth sexy tone said over and over as she replayed the message. He had more faith in her than she had in herself. Why did she give up so easily? Why couldn't she try? The questions flowed through her with the strength of the ocean at high tide. She didn't want to give up either. The knowledge struck her like an electrical shock.

Picking up the phone, she dialed Tabby's number. *I have to try. I have to see if I can face my fears.* She wasn't ready to face Luciano. Who knew if she'd ever be able to. But she needed to face her mom. She needed to give her a chance if she wanted to have any kind of future for herself.

Chapter Fifteen

Kaylee sat in the car, her pale yellow dress hugging her body like a cocoon. Too bad it couldn't protect her as well. Bri and Tabby didn't understand. Anne Daniels would marry another good looking, love 'em and leave 'em type of man like all the others, and she'd be the one who'd have to pick up the pieces when it fell apart.

Kaylee's lungs refused to fill with air. Just the site of the little wedding chapel suffocated her, her ears ringing, her heart racing. A sticky feeling sat in her mouth, coating it, making it hard to open, impossible to speak. What had she been thinking? *Stupid, stupid, stupid. I can't do this.*

"Yes, you can," Tabby said as she parked the car next to the tiny chapel.

"Did I say that out loud?"

"Nope."

Great. Now I'm letting people read me like an open book.

Tabby cut the car's engine and silence rang in her ears. It pounded at her head, urging her to turn around before it was too late. Why had she agreed to do this? What did she hope to get from it? A voice inside her whispered Luciano's name. Somehow, deep inside she wanted this to bring her closer to him. If she put her past to rest, maybe she could have a future with him.

The three girls sat against Tabby's black leather seats without saying a word. Kaylee knew they were letting her compose herself, letting her prepare for facing her demons. She loved them more than ever for it.

Years ago she'd promised herself she'd never support another one of her mom's attempts to find Mr. Right. Stepping into this chapel felt like a concession. She didn't support what her mom did but by walking in the door she threw in the towel. The fight would end before she really had the chance to throw any punches. She'd danced around the ring for a few years, but never actually put herself out there, never let her mom really know how she felt.

And now she would sit in the audience and watch her mom play the happy bride just like a good little girl should. Her mind reverted back to that little girl who once had false hopes. Hopes that maybe this time her mom would be right, that this would be the one, and they'd all live happily ever after.

Finally, she'd learned her lesson. She didn't believe in that dream. Not for herself, and not for her mom, though for the first time she actually wished it could be different. Luciano changed that. Damn him.

"You ready to go in, girl?" Bri's voice intruded her thoughts.

"Yeah." Holding off wouldn't make it any easier. She still had to walk in that door and watch her mom say, I do, to more pain and heartache.

Opening the door the heat from the sun sizzled her skin as she stepped into the unusually hot San Francisco day. Soft music flowed from the open chapel windows pumping her heart to a faster beat. Bri and Tabby each grabbed one of her hands building a fortress around her as they walked inside. To her own surprise she squeezed their hands allowing them to support her. She needed that support now more than ever.

Pale yellow. The flowers decorating the altar, the decorations lining the pews, the announcements handed to her by a man in a black suit at the door were all pale yellow. The same pale yellow of the dress she'd taken hours to pick out. Go figure.

"Look your dress matches," Tabby said with a smile.

Leave it to Tab to find that fact amusing. Kaylee wasn't amused. "Thanks for the news flash, Tab. I kind of noticed that."

"Am I going to have to separate the two of you?" Bri asked. "Since when am I the one getting in the least amount of trouble?"

"You're still the troublemaker of the group. Have no doubt about that." Tabby pulled Kaylee back toward the man standing by the door. "Let's tell him you're the bride's daughter. Maybe he can tell us where your mom is so you can say hi."

Kaylee stopped dead in her tracks, her shoes suddenly held concrete lining. She hadn't expected to see her mom this soon. By cutting the timing so close she hoped Tabby and Bri would just want to find their seats and wait for the ceremony to begin. Of course not. Like things ever went her way. "I don't think we have time. I wouldn't want to make the wedding start late. If I sidetrack her who knows how long it could take." *Good save.*

"Maybe you're right. Plus it will be a nice surprise for your mom to see you when she's walking down the aisle."

Whatever you say, Tabby. "Yeah, a nice surprise. Now can we sit down, please?" Kaylee headed towards the back row. Maybe her mom wouldn't notice her back here. Maybe she would attend this mockery unnoticed.

"Don't think so girl," Bri held her in place. "Family sits in the front."

The wedding march began to play making it impossible to argue with Brianna. Kaylee held her head high and hurried to one of the front aisles with her girls by her side. There were only a few guests littering the pews. Probably about thirty in all. Every one sat staring at the front with huge smiles plastered on their faces as a gentleman who had to be the groom stepped to the front.

He wasn't what she expected.

Where most of the men her mom usually went after had exceptional looks and a bad attitude, this man was your average Joe. He had a slight belly. His hair was thinning on the top with some gray mixed in. His face was rounded with a salt and pepper mustache.

He wasn't anything special except for his smile. He grinned like he was the happiest guy on the planet.

Pure joy shone on his face brighter than the sun. Kaylee stared at her soon to be stepfather. He was everything she didn't expect.

The realization hurt. She didn't want to be so jaded, so negative but how did you change such ingrained feelings and emotions? Was she even strong enough to try? Her eyes locked with the man at the altar. He turned looking at her. His smile brightened as he winked at her. He knew who she was. That much was obvious. His gaze left Kaylee as a creak of the door at the end of the aisle told them someone had entered. His eyes shifted towards the door and exploded with intensity.

Kaylee felt the zap as his eyes found her mom. The gaze sent currents through her. The couple watched each other as Anne walked up the aisle. Kaylee could feel the love flowing between them. Tabby squeezed her hand, and she knew she felt it too. As Anne stepped up to meet her husband to be, the man whispered in her ear and pointed towards Kaylee.

She needed sunglasses for the bright smile her mom shot towards her. Tears glistened visibly in her eyes and Kaylee held back her own. The man obviously loved her mom. He raised his hand to wipe the tears from Anne's face, kissed her cheek, and grabbed her hands as she stood across from him their eyes not seeing anyone but each other.

The ceremony went on, heartfelt and sincere. All the times her mom had been "in love" she never held the look like this. Something grew inside Kaylee as she watched the ceremony. Love, understanding, strength, belief, and hope. Her mom had made plenty of mistakes over the years but this wasn't one of them. She didn't know how but Kaylee knew that just as strongly as she knew she loved Luciano.

Her mom had grown while Kaylee stayed stagnant in the past. Anne braved all the heartache she'd felt in the past and took a leap of faith. She was strong, whole, in love. Her own heart yearned to feel what Anne felt, to brave what her mom did. She wanted that look her mom held in her eyes. She wanted to stand with Luciano hand and hand and not surrender to fear.

All this time she'd been so weak. It was time to change that.

The second Anne and her husband reached the end of the pale yellow flowered aisle Kaylee surged to her feet her excitement fueling her.

"I need the car," she said to Tabby her hand shaking as she held it out. "Hurry I have to go. Can you catch a ride?"

"You bet girl. Go get your man," Bri replied as her and Tabby both hugged Kaylee tightly.

Kaylee turned on her heels running down the aisle her mom just walked down. As she burst through the doors she ran right into her.

"I have to go, Mama. I can't explain now but know I'm so happy for you. Because of you I'm finally ready to go after my own happiness too."

Kaylee kissed her mom on the cheek before turning to run away. "Bye Mom. I love you." She had to get out of there, had to get to *Luciano's* before it was too late.

"Come on, come on," Kaylee said to herself drumming her fingers on the steering wheel. Traffic jammed around her the last block away from *Luciano's*. Her body hummed with excitement and nerves as her heart beat rapidly in her chest. Horns blared, everyone irritated at the stopped traffic.

Spur of the moment, Kaylee pulled into one of the only parking spaces lining the street. In a flash she was out of the car, her feet pounding the pavement as she ran the last of the way to Luciano's. Her nerves out weighed the fear that no doubt still resided inside her.

This is my life, she thought to herself. *I want to be happy.* For the first time in her life she could admit that Bookends wasn't everything. She loved the store, but she loved Luciano too. He was worth the risk to her heart. She was worth going for that chance to be happy, to find love.

Palms sweaty, heart beating on the verge of pumping from her chest, Kaylee pulled open the glass door to *Luciano's* not caring what she looked like. Not caring that she'd just run down the street, sweat dripped from her temple, her braids slipping out of their ponytail. As she rounded the corner she ran smack dab into a firm male wall. Her face buried in the man's chest. One sniff and she knew it was Luciano. His familiar, welcoming, masculine Italian scent enveloped her.

"Bella? Is something wrong?" Luciano's strong hands grasped her shoulders to steady her.

Words escaped her.

She started to cry.

Her heart ached for this man. So many words bombarded her brain. I love you, I'm sorry, I've been so weak, I'm ready to take a chance. The thoughts continued to flow but nothing would leave her lips. He stood there so gorgeous, so beautiful, she couldn't help but remember how his lips felt on hers, how he felt inside her.

Her legs weakened, Kaylee watched the look in Luciano's eyes become more concerned. She couldn't speak. He was so beautiful and all she could do was stare at him. God she loved him so much. Why couldn't she admit it earlier?

"Come on. Let's go into my office." Luciano held her hand leading her back to his office. "What's going on, Kaylee?"

"I...I don't know where to start."

"Start with whatever's on your mind that had you storming in here," Luciano's voice sounded tense. "You haven't initiated any contact with me in weeks and now you barge in, obviously with something important on your mind, but you won't tell me anything."

The walls in Luciano's office began to enclose around them. Closing her eyes and taking a couple deep breaths, Kaylee said, "My mom got remarried today."

Luciano grabbed her hand. The intimate touch somehow eased the vice grip around her voice box. "I wasn't really looking forward to it, but I went."

"I'm glad, Bella—"

"Let me get this out, Luciano. Don't interrupt me for a minute, okay?" she pleaded.

He sat quietly and didn't say a word.

"I sat in the pews ready to cry, ready to run, ready to get up and yell what a joke the wedding was, but then I saw her husband, the compassion in his eyes. He seemed different, different than any man I'd ever seen her with before.

"Then I saw my mom. I saw the looks they exchanged, the smiles on their faces, the love in their eyes. I know it sounds crazy, hell, I don't believe it myself but I felt their connection. It felt almost more real than anything I've ever experienced."

Tears again pricked her eyes but before Kaylee could raise a hand to wipe them, Luciano did the honors for her.

"When I saw their love, at that moment it hit me that despite all the men my mom had in her life just so she could have someone there, she really did love this man. Honestly and truly. The love I saw in his eyes matched hers ten fold.

"That's wonderful, Bella. I'm glad your mom found happiness."

Kaylee cleared her throat so she could continue. "For the first time in her life, I think she really did. And after everything, she deserves it. Everyone does. I do-" she stammered.

A light of understanding lit in Luciano's dark eyes. "What are you saying?"

Kaylee began pacing the room. Somehow the walls that earlier seemed to be closing in on her seemed to stretch out for eternity. The room seemed so big and she felt lost in it. "I'm not very good at this— opening up thing."

Luciano sat quietly not giving her an easy out.

Turning to face him, Kaylee said, "I want to be happy."

"I thought your bookstore made you happy?" Luciano asked fishing.

"It does but not the giddy, butterflies in your stomach, light in your eyes kind of happiness. I didn't even think that existed before today, but it does. And I want it. I don't want to be a coward anymore. Fear led my life for so long, Luciano. I don't want to be afraid anymore."

"What does all this have to do with me?"

Leave it to Luciano to make her spell it out for him. If she wanted him, she'd have to ask for him.

"I want to take a chance—with you. When you told me you loved me, my heart bled for what I wanted so badly but felt I could never have. I've never loved anyone like I love you, Luciano. You laugh with me, sometimes at me," she added with a smile. "You respect me, help me, value my opinion, and understand how important my work is to me. No one gets me like you do and I don't want to let that go."

Luciano made it to his feet and was at Kaylee's side before she could blink. Heat radiated from him, begging her to touch him. Before Kaylee could make the move, Luciano had her in his firm, engulfing embrace.

"Bella," Luciano whispered as he began feathering soft kisses on her neck. "Tell me again."

"I love you, Luciano. Hell, I've probably always loved you. I don't want to be scared anymore. I want to face my future—" Luciano's kisses distracted her. "With you."

Picking her up Luciano moved his hands down to cup her rounded bottom as Kaylee wrapped her legs around his waist. "I love you too, Bella. I love you, too."

Luciano's mouth came down on her waiting lips. His tongue dove into her mouth claiming her. For the first time, Kaylee wanted to be claimed. Each lap of his tongue stirred her soul deep. Their lives merging together as their mouths did.

Pulling away slowly Kaylee tried to speak. "Thank—" Luciano's lips kissed her gently. "You—" again he interrupted her with his mouth. "For—giving—me—another—chance."

"Shh," Luciano replaced his lips with his finger. "Thank you for trusting me, for loving me. I'm so lucky you walked into my life, Bella."

Kaylee laughed. "No, I'm the lucky one. For once in my life, I feel truly lucky."

Luciano led Kaylee from his office their hands entwined. As they rounded the corner into the dining area a large crowd of happy, laughing people stopped to look at the couple entering the room.

"Kaylee?"

"Mama? What are you doing here?" shock etched her words.

"Your friend Tabby helped to book this restaurant for the reception." Anne reached out wrapping her daughter in a warm, motherly hug. "Thank you, baby. Thanks for coming to my wedding."

Kaylee opened her mouth to reply but as if her mom read her thoughts she stopped her. "We don't need to do that, Sweet Pea." Turning to the man beside her she continued, "I'd like you to meet my husband. Kaylee meet Mike. Mike this is my beautiful daughter, Kaylee."

Kaylee stepped into Mike's open arms hugging him, welcoming him before stepping back by Luciano's side.

"Can I ask who this young man is?" her mom asked.

Exhaling a deep, shaky breath, Kaylee looked up at Luciano and then to her mom and her new husband. "This is my…my boyfriend, Luciano." In all her years she'd never uttered those words.

Tears sprang to Anne's eyes, slowly rolling down her cheeks. Luciano smiled before stepping forward to hug Anne. "It's a pleasure to meet you." As they embraced one another, Luciano continued, "You have a wonderful daughter and I want you to know I love her very much."

"You must be a very special man. Kaylee doesn't give her love very freely. I can't wait to get to know you."

Kaylee felt at home as Luciano wrapped his arm around her waist pulling her close. "We're lucky to have found each other."

"I can't believe you did it," Bri interrupted as she and Tabby stormed into their intimate circle. Nico followed behind dressed in his chef whites.

"I'm so happy for you," Tabby said hugging Kaylee first, then Luciano.

"All I can say is it's about damn time," Bri added.

Winking at Kaylee and Luciano before he spoke, Nico said, "Now if I could just get Tabby here to forgive me, maybe we'd be announcing three new couples today."

Sneering at him Tabby said, "Please. Like you even know the meaning of the word relationship. You change women more often than you change the specials at Luciano's. You better go find your woman of the moment before someone bursts in and starts kissing you in the middle of our conversation."

Kaylee looked at her friend, surprised. Obviously something had gone down between Nico and Tabby that she didn't know about.

"Okay, Tab. Today is about the Daniels women and the men in their lives," Bri hooked her arm through Tabby's.

Kissing her on the cheek Mike said, "This beautiful woman is now, Mrs. Thompson."

Everyone oohed and awed. Grabbing Kaylee's hands and turning her to face him, Luciano said, "And I'm hoping this woman will agree to be Mrs. Valenti."

Kaylee's heart stopped as everyone around them hushed to a quick silence. "Don't answer now," Luciano said kissing her lips. "My Mama would kill me if I proposed without a ring. I'm just letting you know what's coming."

Allowing herself to breathe before she passed out Kaylee smiled. She'd never considered getting married, never thought she'd fall in love. Meeting Luciano changed her world in more ways than she could count. Who knew one day she'd be this lucky? Who knew Kaylee Daniels would really be getting lucky with Luciano?

"I'll be looking forward to it," she replied before his lips again met hers.